"I...
mu...

Andrea had replaced the telephone receiver and slowly turned to the rigidly erect figure staring out the window. Her voice cracked with a checked sob. "Please, Tell, let me explain."

"Just answer me this," Tell commanded arrogantly, "was that man on the phone your husband or not?"

"I am legally married to him," Andrea admitted, "but..."

"Then accept the fact that we're through, Andrea." A cold smile was carved into the bronze mask as Tell moved to the door and yanked it open. "Maybe you'll have better luck with your next sucker."

Even before the door had slammed after him, Andrea knew he didn't want to listen to her. But she loved him too desperately not to try again. Somehow she had to make him understand....

JANET DAILEY AMERICANA

TO TELL
THE TRUTH

Harlequin Books

TORONTO • NEW YORK • LONDON
AMSTERDAM • PARIS • SYDNEY • HAMBURG
STOCKHOLM • ATHENS • TOKYO • MILAN
MADRID • WARSAW • BUDAPEST • AUCKLAND

The state flower depicted on the cover of this book is
Oregon grape.

Janet Dailey Americana edition published December 1987
Second printing September 1988
Third printing September 1989
Fourth printing September 1990
Fifth printing November 1991

ISBN 0-373-21937-7

Harlequin Presents edition published May 1978
Second printing May 1980
Third printing February 1982

Original hardcover edition published in 1977
by Mills & Boon Limited

TO TELL THE TRUTH

CHAPTER ONE

THE TAXI TIRES crunched through the plowed streets, snow mounded in high walls on either side. The milk-gray sky blended with the snow-covered slopes of the Sierra Nevada, fat crystalline flakes gently falling from the clouds. A group of skiers walked into the street in front of the taxi, skis in their hands, the tips resting against their shoulders. The driver pushed on the horn and they scampered laughingly out of his way. Then the tire chains clinked to a stop in front of the ski lodge.

"Here you are, miss," the driver announced, and the chill of the December afternoon swept into the warm interior as he opened the door and slid from behind the wheel.

As she stepped from the rear of the taxi and waited on the snow-mounded curb while the driver removed her luggage, Andrea Grant's arrival did not occur without notice, but the interest was only passing curiosity. No one recognized her and she felt a blissful sense of freedom with each breath of mountain air that filled her lungs. An entire week without sly comments being made behind her back, Andrea thought. She hadn't realized the gossip had bothered her.

A smile curved the fullness of her lips. A large flake landed on her nose and she wanted to laugh. How glad she was that John had suggested she take this holiday, the first one that she had had in more than three years.

John, always so wise and understanding, had stepped in to fill her father's shoes when she had so unexpectedly lost him so soon after cancer had taken her mother. He had offered his helping hand again when her engagement to Dale Marshall had been broken. *Face it*, Andrea scolded herself sternly, *Dale jilted you.* But that was in the past. She breathed in deeply. She would not let that bitter memory color her holiday.

The taxi driver was standing on the curb, her suitcases tucked under his arms. Letting the sparkle of anticipation return to her hazel eyes, Andrea turned toward the lodge entrance.

The lobby was crowded with skiers who had called it a day before the cloud-hidden sun settled behind Squaw Peak, the namesake of Squaw Valley. The hum of voices and laughter was nonstop. Andrea noticed that there was a contagion in the easy friendliness that abounded. Her own smile was warmer and more natural as she thanked the driver, adding a generous tip to his fee after he had set her luggage in front of the registration desk.

"It was *my* pleasure," he responded, as his gaze swung admiringly over her figure.

Andrea missed the driver's look, but she saw those directed her way by the male skiers in the lobby. She ignored them as she ignored all the other looks that had come her way since Dale.

That faint air of aloofness only increased her attraction, although it did succeed in keeping men at arm's length. She was fair-complexioned, but there was no coolness to her beauty. Wide and bright hazel eyes were heavily fringed with lashes and flecked with a warm olive green. Dark blond hair was swept away from her face, its shiny medium length swirling into thick curls angling away from her ears and neck for an attractive windblown effect. There was a model's uniqueness rather than perfection to her prominent cheekbones, although her figure was more curved than the pencil thinness of a model's.

"May I help you, miss?" The tightly polite line of the desk clerk's mouth relaxed into a smile.

"Yes, I believe you have a reservation for me. Andrea Grant," she supplied.

Flipping part way through a card index, he stopped. "Andrea Grant from Oregon. We have your reservation right here for one of the apartments. You'll be staying with us for a week, is that right?" At her answering nod, he smiled and slid a registration slip and pen toward her. "Fill this out, please, and I'll find someone to help you with your luggage."

Not an easy task, Andrea thought to herself as the clerk's attention was immediately claimed by a family waiting to register behind her. With her head bent over the registration form, she became conscious of being watched. She glanced to the side, and encountered the alertly appraising look of a pair of brown, nearly black eyes. The lean, handsome face revealed little concern that he had been caught studying her.

"Hello." His low husky voice vibrated around her.

Black hair gleamed with melted snowflakes while

amusement deepened the creases along the corners of his mouth. Slightly nonplussed, Andrea stared into the strongly masculine face, feeling the leap of physical response to his unquestionable attraction. What was more, he knew her reaction, or sensed it at least.

Andrea guessed that his virile charm had breached the walls of a lot more than one feminine citadel.

"Hello." She returned the greeting evenly and reverted her attention to the form.

"May I have my key, Mike?" The request was addressed to the desk clerk as the man observed Andrea's subtle hint that she didn't wish to indulge in any idle flirtation.

"Sure thing, Mr. Stafford. There's a message for you, too." The key and a slip of paper were placed on the counter.

The hand that reached past Andrea was brown and strong. A brief, sideways glance at his face caught a thoughtful expression. That recklessly attractive look had vanished. He cast not one look her way as he moved away from the desk. She watched him leave, taking note of his tallness and his deceptively lean build that tapered wide shoulders into slim hips.

Something in the way he carried himself rang a bell in her memory. For a second Andrea couldn't place what it was; then she remembered the time several years ago when her father had pointed out a well-known figure. "Do you see the way he holds his head and those firm, unhurried strides?" he had asked. "There's a man who has earned the right to command and is respected immediately by all those people whom he commands."

Mr. Stafford, the desk clerk had called him. The name wasn't familiar to Andrea, but she hadn't really expected it to be. There was more than surface charm to the man and she wished now that she had not been quite so aloof. She would have liked to find out more about him. Only for curiosity's sake, she assured herself. She wasn't interested in him as a man.

Then her view of the disappearing stranger was blocked by a young man with two of her bags tucked under one arm as he reached for the key from the desk clerk. The informal atmosphere of the ski lodge was enhanced by the lack of uniforms on the staff, but Andrea guessed that this was the bellboy in his stag's head sweater and brown slacks.

"Art will show you to your room," the desk clerk told her as she slid the completed registration form to him.

"Could you recommend a restaurant?" Andrea requested.

"There're several in the Olympic House ranging from a steak house to sandwich or pizza shops. All of them serve good food. It all depends on what you want." He shrugged.

"Thank you," she said with a smile. "I think I'll decide after I unpack."

The accommodation was more spacious than she required, but it had been the only thing available when she had made the booking. Andrea decided that before the week was out she would probably be grateful for the relative privacy and comfort of the living room with its fully equipped kitchenette and the separate bedroom loft.

The memories it brought back of previous vacations at Squaw Valley with her parents, staying in a room very similar to this one, were happy memories. Most of the grief she had felt at the deaths following so closely on one another was gone now. She could look back without pain and sorrow.

Time was a healer. She could even think of Dale now without wanting to dissolve into tears. She knew part of her bitterness had been because his defection had followed so closely on the heels of her father's death. She had barely recovered from the shock of it when he had left her.

John had told her that he had once loved and lost himself, but he had recovered. He had assured her that there would be a time when she would trust again and love again. Andrea wasn't nearly so certain. True, there had been moments recently when she had wanted a man's arms around her and his kiss on her lips. But they were physical desires, born of natural instinct.

Mentally she shied away from men, unwilling to feel that deep, abiding hurt again. No one she had met had possessed John's strength of character she so admired or the feeling she could depend on him no matter what. How very lucky she had been that her father had possessed a friend like John.

Partially unpacked, Andrea left the opened suitcases on her bed and walked swiftly to the telephone. John would be worrying about whether she had arrived safely. She gave the operator the number in Oregon, and her fingers tapped impatiently on the table. The housekeeper answered on the second ring.

"Mrs. Davison, this is Andrea. May I speak to John?"

"He's in his study ... waiting for you to phone." The Housekeeper's hesitation before adding the last phrase increased the impression of reproval at Andrea's tardiness. Before Andrea could explain that she hadn't even unpacked, John's voice came over the line.

"Andie, I was wondering when you'd call. I was beginning to get uneasy." He seemed to reach across the wires and take hold of her hand, the warmth and gladness in his greeting lightening her own heart.

"I arrived safely, John. I'd started to unpack and decided to call you first. It's so beautiful here. There's fresh snow falling and everything is so pure and white, like a Christmas-card scene. You would love it. I wish you'd come." Her enthusiasm ended on a wistful note.

"I'm too old to keep up with you, Andie," he said, laughing.

"Will you stop harping about how old you are?" Andrea scolded lightly.

"I am old. Much older than you."

Behind his humorous tone, she caught the note of seriousness. Immediately a picture sprang to mind of him sitting behind the large walnut desk in his study, backed by shelves of bound books and richly paneled walls. His hair was dark brown but the sideburns were frosted with silver. The touch of gray made him look distinguished, not old. He had a wide powerful jaw, a cleft in his chin and warm gray eyes.

11

"Do you know —" Andrea laughed back the lump in her throat "— I think I'm getting homesick?"

"Nonsense! I heard that initial spurt of excitement in your voice. This vacation is going to do you a world of good. We both know you were letting the talk from some small minds get to you. You needed to get away."

She smiled into the receiver. "You're right as usual. You're so wise, John," she sighed.

"I wish I was always as positive about that as you seem to be," he observed dryly.

"I still miss you," Andrea stated, deliberately making her voice light.

"Maybe you won't be so anxious to rush back when I tell you that I finished another chapter today," he said. "Thanks to your research notes, I'll probably have several more ready for you to type when you get back."

"I wonder if I can find accommodation for another week," she said, responding in kind to his teasing remarks.

"Are you handing in your notice as my typist, my personal Girl Friday and my right arm?" John said, laughing.

"A week of sun and snow and skiing will be all I'll want," she assured him.

"Telephone once in a while so I won't start imagining you with a cast on your leg."

"I will, I promise."

"Enjoy yourself, Andie. Be young and foolish while you can."

"At twenty-two, I sincerely hope I'm past that stage,"

Andrea answered, more sharply than she had intended.

"Yes, you are very nearly over the hill, aren't you?" But John didn't allow her an opportunity to respond to his mocking observation. "Have a good time, honey."

"I will ... and take care of yourself."

There was a tightness in her throat when Andrea hung up the telephone. She refused to give in to the cold finger of apprehension that ran down her spine. It was senseless to feel this odd depression. John wanted her to enjoy this holiday, and certainly she did.

In a flurry of activity. Andrea finished unpacking, bathed and changed. Forsaking the standard sweater and slacks, she chose a camel-tan tunic and matching, wide-legged pants. A cream-colored silk blouse added a dressy touch to the outfit. She considered wearing the owl locket John had given her before deciding on a gold braided chain necklace. Her suede parka was the same camel shade as her outfit.

Outdoors, the mountain air sharply revived her appetite, reminding her that she had not eaten since late morning. Walking alone while everyone else was in pairs or groups, Andrea avoided the more crowded restaurants, choosing the steak house in the Olympic House where her solitary state might not be so noticeable. The last thing she wanted was to fend off some man's advances the first night she was there.

Like nearly all the other eating establishments, the steak house was crowded. Andrea waited at the front entrance while the host seated the couple who had been ahead of her. She was vaguely aware of someone enter-

13

ing the restaurant and stopping behind her. Since she knew no one, Andrea didn't bother to glance around.

"Well, we meet again," a familiar voice said.

A startled look over her shoulder encountered the stranger she had seen at the desk, the Mr. Stafford who had aroused her curiosity for a moment. The ski suit was gone, replaced by a white ribbed turtleneck sweater and a dark blazer. If anything, his looks were more arresting than before, especially in view of the singularly attractive smile that softened his lean, chiseled features.

"Hello." Andrea inclined her dark blond head in acknowledgment.

"Have you settled in for the weekend?"

She nearly explained to him that she would be staying a week, then decided it wasn't necessary. "Yes, I have, thank you."

"Hi, Tell. How are you tonight?" The host approached, smiling widely at the man standing behind Andrea.

"Just fine, Kyle," the man answered.

"I have a table for the two of you right over here." The host started to walk away and Andrea realized that he assumed she was with Mr. Stafford.

She hastened to correct his error. "Excuse me, but we aren't together."

The restaurateur halted, tilting his head curiously to the side while a bewildered expression crossed his face, his eyes darting from Andrea to the man next to her. "Do you mean you want two tables for one?"

Out of the corner of her eye she could see Mr. Stafford

was not going to be of any assistance. He seemed to find her quickness in making certain that the man realized they were not together secretly amusing.

"Yes," she said.

"Two tables for one does sound a bit ridiculous," the man named Stafford said softly. "Would you join me for dinner? It would be a pleasure, I assure you."

Andres hesitated. The restaurant was crowded and curiosity still lingered. There was no harm in eating at the same table with this man.

"Yes, thank you." She smiled faintly.

Their host's smile mirrored an inner satisfaction as he led them to the table. He held the chair out for Andrea while Mr. Stafford took the one opposite.

"I'm sorry," her dinner companion said after they had been left to study the menus. His hand reached across the table to her. "I neglected to introduce myself. Tell Stafford is the name, from San Francisco."

"Andrea Grant." The firm clasp of his handshake eased the tension she hadn't been aware existed until it left.

"From California?"

"No, Oregon, originally," she answered. "Everyone here seems to know you. You must come to Squaw Valley quite often, Mr. Stafford."

"Tell," he corrected, adding with persuasive insistence, "please. Actually, it's Tellman but fortunately it's shortened to Tell. It was my mother's maiden name. May I call you Andrea?" At her nod of agreement, he continued, "I come to Squaw Valley as often as I can. Of late, it hasn't been as frequent as I would like it to be."

"What do you do?" she asked.

"My family owns a small chain of department stores in the Bay area," Tell Stafford answered easily, but there was a faint narrowing of his eyes that suggested he was judging her reaction. "And what about you?"

"I've been doing research and manuscript typing on a novel." Why in the world had she told him that, Andrea asked herself. It was too late to retract it now. She had to let it stand.

"For a writer?"

"The book hasn't actually been accepted yet. It's his first attempt at that length, but he does have a publisher interested in it," Andrea explained.

To her relief the waiter arrived to take their order. She had barely had time to look at the menu, so she allowed Tell Stafford to make his recommendations.

"Wine?" he questioned after inquiring how she liked her steak.

"Nothing alcoholic, thank you. Milk, please," she told the waiter.

During the meal, the conversation shifted to general topics. Tell Stafford was very adept at what might be described as table talk, Andrea learned. He answered each question she put to him, yet when their coffee was served, she felt no nearer to discovering what there was about him that fascinated her. She would have been less than honest if she hadn't admitted that she found his dark looks attractive.

16

All in all, she had learned a great deal about him yet knew nothing. He was in his early thirties, unmarried, intelligent and possessed a keen sense of humor. His confidence was unshakable. But the knowledge was all superficial. The sensation persisted that he had learned more about her than she had about him.

"What's troubling you, Andrea?" He was leaning back in his chair, his head tipped to one side.

Guiltily, her hazel eyes bounced away from him, aware that her contemplative silence had stretched longer than she had realized. She started to deny that there was any basis for his question, then laughed and answered honestly.

"We've been talking for almost an hour, yet I have the feeling that I don't know you at all."

"That makes two of us." Tell smiled and Andrea liked the way his eyes crinkled at the corners. "Since the first time I saw you in the lobby, I thought there was something different about you. I've finally come to the conclusion that you don't have the attitude of a predator."

"A predator?" Andrea frowned with amusement.

"I've been stalked a few times, Andrea." The dark eyes sparkled across the table at her, his expression displaying no false modesty, nor was it bragging. She had never doubted that women found him physically attractive. She had, too, so his statement came as no surprise. "The stealth and cunning of a female is not something I admire in your sex. My mother claims that my chauvinistic side insists on doing the hunting."

17

"I see." His explanation disconcerted her. It was one thing to view him as a man who aroused her curiosity. Only in a most abstract way did she want to look on him as a potential lover. "You rarely mention your father. Is he alive?"

The corners of his mouth twisted upward, not into a smile because it didn't reach his eyes the way Andrea was by then accustomed to seeing.

"You're doing it again. Each time there's any mention of a man-woman relationship on a personal level, you veer away from it and onto another subject. But to answer your question, my father was killed in a car accident when I was about ten. My mother has since remarried to a very understanding man. He and I are good friends."

"That's good." Andrea smiled brightly. "Sometimes there's resentment when a parent remarries."

"You're not basically a shy woman, Andrea," Tell observed, studying the wariness that sprang into her face as he reintroduced his previous topic. "It isn't any embarrassment on your part concerning the sexual relationship. Yet I have the impression that you're determined to keep a certain amount of distance between us. You'll let me get just so close and no closer. Why the invisible barrier?"

The waiter arrived with their check, enabling Andrea to evade his question. When she insisted on paying for her own meal, refusal darkened his lean features. Then with an arched black brow and a mocking curve to his mouth, Tell relented, accepting the money she handed him. When they rose from the table, his hand closed over her elbow.

"I'll walk you to the lodge," he stated.

"That isn't necessary," Andrea protested.

But one glance at the resolute line of his jaw told her that in this he wouldn't yield. She was beginning to learn that he was a man who knew what he wanted to do and did it. No one stood in his way unless he allowed it.

The night sky was still spitting snow, the tiny flakes making a light film on the sidewalk. The firm grip on her elbow had relaxed, but she could still feel the touch of his hand through her lined parka. Their silence seemed out of tune with the laughter and voices of the other skiers traversing the square.

"Were you very much in love with him?" The silence was shattered by his softly spoken question.

"Who?" Andrea stalled, glancing at Tell in false bewilderment. But the dark, knowing eyes weren't fooled.

"The man who's made you so afraid of becoming involved again," he answered calmly and confidently.

Staring straight ahead, Andrea neither admitted nor denied his observation. His perception was unnerving. She wished now that she had never accepted his invitation to dine at his table.

"You must have been very much in love with him," he concluded from her silence. "Was he married?"

There was anger in the glance she darted upward to his face, a resentment that he should continue to probe a wound that was so obviously still painful. He met her look and returned it, letting Andrea see that he wouldn't

19

be put off by her silence—he demanded a response.

"No, he wasn't married," she answered tightly. "We were engaged. A month before our wedding he decided he cared for someone else."

"When was this?"

A breeze swirled around the corner of a building, sending a light curl across her cheek. She pushed it from her face with impatient irritation.

"Three years ago," was her stilted response.

"That's about the time you told me you lost your father," Tell remarked thoughtfully. "And your mother several months before that. The pain didn't seem to stop, did it?"

Keeping her chin at a defiant angle, Andrea rejected any sympathy or pity from him. But there was none mirrored in his tanned face as he reached past her to open the lodge door.

"It happens that way sometimes," he said, shrugging philosophically. "Do you have the key to your room?"

"Yes." Andrea produced it from her leather purse as his hand again touched her elbow.

"You mentioned that you and your parents came to Squaw Valley quite often in the winter. You must have a lot of happy memories here," he commented.

She almost breathed her relief aloud at the change of subject. It was strange the way the tables had turned. At dinner she had set out to find out about this tall stranger. Instead he was the one who was finding out about her private life.

"Yes, many memories," she agreed.

At the door to her room, Tell Stafford took the key and unlocked the door, handing the key back to her after he had pushed the door open.

"I haven't thanked you for sharing my table with me. I enjoyed your company."

He offered his hand and Andrea again felt the firm warmth of his grip. There was a dark sparkle in his gaze. She couldn't be certain, but she thought it was from amusement at the vaguely tense smile she gave him in return.

"Yes, thank you, Tell," she said stiffly.

"I'll probably see you somewhere on the slopes tomorrow," was his casual goodbye.

CHAPTER TWO

AT THE END of her second run down Bailey's Beach, Andrea recognized the carnelian-colored ski-suited man waiting on the bottom. Sun goggles concealed the direction of Tell Stafford's gaze but he raised a ski pole in greeting as she approached.

In a way, she hadn't expected him to seek her out today, not after the resentment she had shown him last night. Not that it mattered, she told herself. She wasn't interested in him or anyone as a romantic companion for her holiday. But there was a traitorous burst of warmth in her veins at the smile that flashed across the masculine mouth.

"Are you ready to leave the gentler slopes behind for something more demanding?" he challenged as she stopped beside him.

"What did you have in mind?" The breathy catch to her voice was caused by the high altitude, Andrea told herself.

Are you up to KT-22?"

"I think so," she said, nodding.

"Let's go." Tell dug his poles into the snow and pushed off towards the chair-lift that would take them to the famous Olympic hill.

It was a test of mettle that required a complete recall of all her former skill to keep up with Tell's slicing skis.

She had guessed that he was an expert skier, but she had expected him to consider the years since her last time on skis and choose a route accordingly. He spared neither himself nor her.

The exhilaration that accompanied the successful completion of the run was beyond anything Andrea had experienced. Her senses were vibrantly alive to everything around her. It was like awakening after a long, troubled sleep and finding a fresh new world. She didn't need a second invitation to return up the slopes.

By the end of the afternoon, Andrea was happily exhausted. She had taken a couple of tumbles and knew there would probably be bruises, as well as stiff muscles, making themselves felt by morning but she couldn't remember when she had felt so complete and whole.

"I'll give you an hour in the tub to soak out the soreness and another half an hour to dress," Tell stated with that smile that had added to the bewitching spell of the afternoon, "then I'll expect you in the lobby. No more time than that, because I'm starving."

"I'll be there," she promised gaily as they parted in the hallway, Andrea walking toward her room and Tell to his.

Not until she was lazing in a tubful of soothing bubbles did she realize that she had agreed to dine with him. Disobeying the warning voices that pleaded with her to stay away from him, she sighed contentedly. Except for that one moment last night, she had enjoyed his company.

She was beginning to feel alive again and it wasn't as

23

frightening as she had thought. In fact, it was a wonderful feeling, she decided, picking up a handful of bubbles and blowing them into the air.

A lot of girls indulged in harmless flirtations. Why shouldn't she? Andrea argued silently. True, she hadn't come with that in mind, but where would she ever find a better holiday companion than Tell Stafford? He was good-looking, fun, maybe too worldly for her, but it would be exciting. She had lived on the fringe of life for three years. It was her turn to enjoy it.

In this faintly euphoric state where nothing could possibly go wrong, Andrea dressed for her date with Tell. A date ... even that word brought a smile. She hadn't had a date in years. A glow of excitement radiated from within as she hurried to the lobby to meet Tell.

When his dark gaze ran admiringly over her slimly curvaceous figure, there was a surge of satisfaction in knowing how well the brown slacks and the matching gold and brown striped sweater suited her coloring. Minus the wariness that had held her distant the night before, Andrea found herself willingly following his lead. The lightest touch sent new fires of life through her system.

After eating at one of the more informal spots, Tell didn't take her back to the lodge. "Will your legs take a couple of hours of dancing, or are you too sore?" There was a glitter of laughter in his eyes as he looked down at her.

"I don't feel the least bit tired," Andrea admitted, "although I can't say how coordinated my legs will be. I can't remember how long it's been since I had as much exercise as I did this afternoon."

His arm slipped around her shoulders as he turned her into one of the lounges. "We probably should have called it a day earlier."

"I'm not complaining." She shook her head firmly and smiled. "I wouldn't have changed anything today. It was all magnificent."

"I thought it was, too." There was a promise of something else in his low, husky voice.

Somehow, Tell succeeded in finding an empty table in one corner of the crowded lounge. The possessive touch of his hands on her shoulders kept her firmly in front of him, making certain that they weren't accidentally separated in the jostling group of people. A bearded waiter in the perennial sweater and slacks was at their table within seconds.

"What'll you have?" the man asked with a faintly impatient look.

"A Coke," Andrea responded quickly.

"A Coke and what, lady?" the waiter asked, the line of his mouth thinning out.

"A plain Coke. Nothing else," she explained.

With a raised eyebrow he turned to Tell. "And you?"

"Scotch and water." As the waiter departed, Tell let his lazy, contemplative gaze swing to Andrea. "You actually don't drink, do you?"

"I've heard that liquor is an acquired taste. I simply haven't acquired the taste." There was a defensive shrug

25

to her shoulders. "And I'm not really interested in trying. I'd rather get high on a Sierra sunset."

"There's no need to be embarrassed about it," Tell said gently.

"I'm not . . ." Then Andrea smiled at herself and nodded ruefully at him. "I suppose I am self-conscious about it."

"And defensive." His mouth quirked mockingly.

"And defensive," she admitted with a laugh.

The fingers of one hand had been nervously twirling the ashtray in the center of the small round table. Tell leaned forward, stopping the action as he covered her hand with his.

"Then stop it," he commanded softly.

The warmth of his hand traveled up her arm and down her spine, melting the stiffness with which she had been holding herself. His dark eyes held her gaze. At the moment, the pull of his virile attraction was more heady than any drink could have been. Then the waiter arrived with their drinks and her hand was released as Tell sat back in his chair.

The disturbed cadence of her heart refused to return to normal. Andrea was glad of the few moments of silence that followed the arrival of their drinks. It was one thing to respond to his attention and quite another to be carried away by it.

"Hey, Tell, how are you?" The voice broke into the silence as a hand clasped Tell's shoulder in greeting.

There was a scrape of a chair leg and a tall, slender man was sitting himself down at their table. His face was

26

bronzed to a teak shade by the winter sun and his hair was bleached a wheat gold.

"Hello, Chris." Tell's mouth curved upwards, a cynical hardness deepening the grooves in his cheeks. "Why don't you join us?" he mocked.

"You know me, Tell," the man returned, his blue gaze turning to Andrea, "I never wait for an invitation. I haven't seen you around before, have I, beautiful face?"

"You're getting slow, Chris. She arrived yesterday." The coolness in Tell's voice surprised Andrea and she returned the stranger's look warily, darting a questioning glance at Tell. "Andrea, this is Chris Christiansen, one of the ski instructors here. Andrea Grant," he introduced.

"Andrea," the man repeated her name. "That's a beautiful name, Andrea. It belongs to a beautiful woman. How about a dance?"

"She's with me," Tell said firmly before Andrea had a chance to answer.

There was a measured glance at Tell, then the admiring blue eyes were directed at Andrea. "Is that right?" Chris asked, letting his voice and eyes caress her.

"Yes, that's right," she replied evenly, completely unmoved by his attention, but a warmth radiated through her when Tell's dark gaze burned over her.

"Well—" there was a sighing shrug as Chris rose to his feet, still gazing down at her "—if you change your mind, beautiful face, and decide you want another teacher, I'm always around. See you, Tell."

27

As he disappeared into the crowd, Andrea's hand was taken in a vice-like grip and she was pulled to her feet as Tell rose. "Let's dance," he ordered, a tightness in his brief smile.

They were barely on the small dance floor before he turned her into his arms. There was little room to maneuver in the crowded area. Held closely against him, Andrea didn't object to the crush. She liked the hard circle of his arms and the broad shoulders on which to rest her head. But she didn't submit to that pleasure immediately.

Tilting her head back, she gazed at the uncompromising set of his mouth inches above her. "I didn't know you taught skiing," she murmured curiously.

"What?" Tell frowned.

"Chris said if I wanted another teacher..." Andrea started to explain.

A low chuckle came from his throat, tiny lines crinkling the corners of his eyes. "He was referring to love, not skiing, as the subject."

Andrea self-consciously bit her lower lip and stared at the blue cashmere pullover rather than at the face of its wearer. "I didn't understand."

"I'm glad." The arm around her waist tightened as he gently nuzzled the side of her dark blond hair. She didn't feel foolish any more for not catching the implication of the man's statement.

It was difficult to leave the intoxicating circle of his arms when the song ended. Her awareness of him physically was increasing with each passing minute. Her voice

28

automatically responded to his conversation, but her thoughts were strictly of him, wondering if he too felt the tremors that she did when he touched her or held her. Probably not, she decided wistfully.

This was only a holiday romance ... an enjoyable way of passing the time. Tell found her physically attractive, but it ended there, the same as it did with her. Andrea didn't regret this. Under the circumstances, it was the best thing. At least Tell had enabled her to break free from the chains of the past. Maybe she would never love again as completely and innocently as she had loved Dale, but she was certain now that she didn't want to keep love out of the rest of her life. John would be so glad to hear that, she thought.

"Are you falling asleep on me?" Tell tipped his head back to gaze into her face.

"No, just thinking," Andrea murmured, smiling lazily into the chiseled, handsome lines of his face.

"It's late. You must be exhausted." The song ended and Tell pointed her toward the door. "I'd better take you back to the lodge."

They did not hurry their steps. Reluctantly, Andrea handed him the key to her room, unwilling to have the magic day end. As he had the night before, Tell opened the door and handed the key back to her. She couldn't bring herself to voice the word of good night. Gazing at him, Andrea wasn't aware of the slight pressure of his hands that drew her into his arms. It seemed that she went of her own volition.

Pliantly, she yielded to his probing kiss. There was

hunger in her response, her fingers curled into the raven smoothness of the hair that grew low on his neck. Immediately, his mouth became hard and demanding against hers. Then she felt the undertow of desire sweeping away her control.

While she still had the will, Andrea turned her mouth away from his. The fires were not so easily banked as he buried his head in the soft curve of her neck. She moaned softly in reluctant protest to the havoc within.

"Tell, please," she whispered.

"Invite me in for coffee," he demanded hoarsely, nibbling sharply at the lobe of her ear.

"I don't think so," Andrea said, exhaling with shaky slowness.

Taking a deep breath, Tell slowly lifted his head, cupping her face with his hands. The sensually masculine mouth curved into an excitingly handsome, rueful smile.

"Why am I letting you get away with saying 'no'?" he mused rhetorically.

"Maybe it's because you so seldom hear it," she smiled weakly, knowing with a flash of intuition that she was right.

"You're dangerous, Andrea." A mask stole over his face, making his expression unreadable.

"Me?" she laughed in disbelief. At this moment she felt completely under his domination.

"Yes. I can't make up my mind if you're slipping away from me or closing in for the kill," Tell murmured evenly, and Andrea winced at the underlying tone of harsh cynicism. "I'm sorry," he sighed, brushing a dark

30

golden curl behind her ear. "I can't help being wary. I've been disillusioned too many times. What time are you leaving tomorrow?"

"For where?" Her hazel eyes widened in bewilderment.

"For wherever it is that you live in Oregon?" He mocked her confusion with a twisting smile.

"I'm not leaving tomorrow; not until Friday morning," she told him, remembering how she had let him believe that first night that she would only be at Squaw Valley for the weekend.

"Why didn't you tell me?" His gaze became forbiddingly dark and narrow.

"At the time," Andrea wavered, intimidated by that glimpse of anger and her own instinct that said he could be brutally ruthless. "At the time, it didn't seem important. I didn't even really know you."

"No," Tell agreed. A teasing glitter sparkled through his eyes with a mercurial change of mood. "I was just some arrogant stranger making a pass at you, wasn't I? You can be cool, Andrea." He tantalizingly brushed his hard male mouth against her lips. "And very warm, too. Have breakfast with me tomorrow? I'll phone you around seven."

"Yes." It hadn't been a request, more like an order, but Andrea accepted it anyway. He wished her good night, placed a firm kiss on her mouth and turned away. "Tell?" she called to him hesitantly. He stopped a few steps away but didn't walk back. "When are you leaving?"

31

"I don't have to be back until Wednesday," he told her. "That doesn't give us very much time, does it?"

There was a thoughtfully serious arching of a dark brow, then he turned and walked away. This time she didn't call him back.

Wednesday morning he would go out of her life. She had known he would some time, Andrea reminded herself, so it was insane to feel depressed at knowing exactly when that would be. It was only a holiday thing. The more she repeated that, the larger her doubts loomed.

The vague depression vanished with the sound of Tell's voice on the phone the next morning. There was no time to feel blue. Blue was the color of the Sierra sky. There was too much perfection in the day for Andrea to worry about the "maybe" of tomorrow.

The sun was a gigantic gold nugget suspended above the Mother Lode country, the granite majesty of the Sierra Nevada range. The sky was a brilliant, cloudless blue, casting pastel shadows on the pure white snow of the mountains and valleys. Near the summit of Squaw Peak, the sapphire blue of Lake Tahoe, the Lake in the sky, could be seen ringed by a circlet of white mountains. To the north was Donner pass and the place of encampment for the Donner party. The day was too beautiful to dwell on that pioneer tragedy.

Not even the other skiers on the slopes could disturb the enchanted circle that had drawn Andrea and Tell together. They jointly stretched out each moment, taking their time going down the slopes and eating a late lunch at the restaurant at the top of the gondola lift. In the later afternoon, they sat in front of a fireplace and laughed as Tell tried to teach Andrea to play backgammon, ultimately with some success.

But again the precious seconds of the day slipped by. They were in the hallway outside her room, a midnight sky sparkling with stars beyond the roof of the lodge. There was no mention of coffee or when the other would be leaving. Yet for Andrea, it was there, adding an urgency to the embrace they shared.

When he had left, it was the mirror in her room that brought Andrea crashing back to reality. The soft radiance in her reflection caught at her breath. Her lips were slightly swollen by the frustrated passion of Tell's kisses, bruising in their mastery. A haunted look replaced the jade sparkle in her hazel eyes.

"So you thought you could handle a holiday flirtation?" the mirror mocked. "So you thought you could play with matches and escape the flame? You were so confident that it would be fun and excitement and end with no regrets."

"That's the way it will be," Andrea whispered, choked by the lump in her throat.

"Then why are you falling in love with him?" her reflection jeered. "And why haven't you told him the truth about yourself? What's his opinion of you going to be when he finds out? You're a fool, Andrea Grant!"

Closing her eyes tightly in pain, she turned away from the mirror, knowing that when she opened them nothing would have changed. The truth would be still staring her in the face. What goes up, must come down, she laughed

33

bitterly. And she had been riding high, foolishly thinking that she still had her feet on the ground.

Tell the truth. Wait. Tell the truth. Wait. The two thoughts hammered in her mind, the pounding dilemma making her sleep fitful and plagued with nightmares. She was no nearer to a decision with the rising of the sun.

Once in Tell's presence, the little courage she had mustered vanished over the breakfast table. She couldn't tell him. Andrea wanted another day of happiness in her grasp. It didn't do any good to tell herself that she was not only a fool but selfish as well. So she waited.

"I've made reservations for one of the dinner shows at the casino tonight," Tell told her as they checked in their skis after an afternoon run. "I hope you brought along something halfway formal to wear. If not, we'll run into town and buy something."

"No, I ... I have a dress," Andrea assured him quickly. The prospect of Tell helping to pick out a gown was more painful than pleasing. "What time?"

"Six?" He glanced inquiringly at her, a caressive light in his dark eyes as he reached around her to open the lodge door. "Can you be ready by then?"

"Easily," she said smiling, as she walked with him to the desk to pick up her key.

"You have a message, too, miss," the clerk said, handing her a slip of paper with the key. "He called about a half an hour ago."

Without looking at it, Andrea shoved the message in the pocket of her jacket. Out of the corner of her eyes, she saw the glistening of the overhead light on the raven

34

sheen of Tell's black hair as he tilted his head inquiringly toward her.

"Aren't you even going to see who it's from?" he asked curiously, a watchful glitter in his look.

Self-consciously, she took it from her pocket and glanced at it. She had already guessed it was from John. She had thoughtlessly not called him as she had promised.

"It's ... it's just from John." She shrugged nervously, trying to indicate that it wasn't important.

"And who is John? A boyfriend you have tucked away in Oregon? Is that it?" Tell inquired with false lightness.

"He isn't a boyfriend." Andrea breathed in deeply. The message clutched in her hand could be the means to begin telling him the truth.

A slow smile began to curve his mouth. "He's the writer you've been working for, isn't he?" At her faint nod, he reached out and took the paper from her fingers. "A message from an employer invariably is a call back to work."

"Tell!" she gasped, recovering from her stunned surprise and reaching out to take back the message. But he easily eluded her attempt.

"If you didn't receive the message, then you can't know he called. And you won't have received any summons to go back to work." Deliberately, he tore the paper into tiny bits and tossed it into a nearby wastebasket.

"You shouldn't have done that," Andrea breathed,

her gaze swinging from the metal basket to meet his glittering gaze. "But I'm glad you did."

"If you're going to be ready by six," he glanced at his gold wristwatch, "you'd better get started."

"I'll be ready and waiting," she promised.

Three times in her room, she picked up the telephone to call John, but each time she replaced the receiver. Andrea couldn't understand her own hesitancy. There was a vague premonition that the next time she heard John's voice, the walls would come crashing down around her. It was a crazy sensation, but she couldn't overcome it. And the knowledge that Tell would be arriving at six easily allowed her to put off phoning until the next day.

THE ROAD FOLLOWED the twisting, turning shoreline of Lake Tahoe, its jewel colors hidden by a coat of black satin that matched the night sky. Tall pines stretched upward on the forested slopes of the mountains, their green limbs cloaked in white snow. A smattering of stars winked in the sky waiting for the moon to make its entrance.

The show they were attending was at one of the casinos on the south shore of Lake Tahoe, naturally on the Nevada side. Their circuitous route on the snow-packed, curving road took more time than the miles indicated, but Andrea didn't mind. It was the first time she and Tell had been truly alone and she enjoyed the quiet intimacy which they shared as they rode along in the car.

By silent mutual consent, they talked of abstract

36

things: of weather, politics, and sport. Sometimes, they said nothing at all. It was a disappointment to Andrea when the lights of the casinos blinked their neon colors in front of them. She hadn't wanted the drive to end yet.

Inside the plushly decorated gambling casino, the din of the slot machines was never ending, increased by the voice of the players at the tables. It seemed crowded to her, but Tell said it wasn't. The seating had begun for the dinner show, so he promised to take her around the casino afterwards since this was her first visit. She enjoyed the name entertainment, but she was more conscious of the arm lying naturally around her shoulders than the songs being sung on the stage.

Afterward, as Tell had promised, he took her around the various gaming tables. Under his tutelage, she placed a bet at the wheel of fortune and won, with the same result at the roulette wheel. At the dice tables, the action was too swift for her to follow, so it was Tell who placed the bet and won. His luck remained the same at the twenty-one tables. This time he let his winnings ride and the stack of chips kept increasing. Finally, when he reached the table limit, he cashed in his chips with a frown.

"What's wrong?" Andrea questioned, studying the uncompromising hardness of his expression.

Dark eyes bored into her for a moment before the lines softened into a mocking look. "I just discovered I was superstitious," Tell replied, circling her waist with his arm and turning her away from the tables.

"Superstitious about what?" She laughed softly.

"Lucky at cards, unlucky in love." The fire that blazed over her face made her heart leap in answer. "We haven't lost a bet tonight. I would rather have lost it all," Tell murmured thoughtfully. His words brought the haunted look back to her wide hazel eyes. "I didn't mean to frighten you. There's nothing to that old saying anyway," he scolded in an amused voice. "Now, where would you like to go next? Do you want to try the slot machines?"

"I'd like to leave," Andrea replied quickly.

"Because of what I said?" He tipped his head to the side in regret.

"Partly," she admitted. Her gaze fell away from his tanned face, knowing the other reason was the steadily gnawing fear that had begun the night before. But she tried to make light of it. "And partly because the noise is getting to me and my head."

He nodded an understanding agreement and turned toward the exit door.

They didn't speak again until they had left behind the lights of the motel and residential district on the south shore. Then Tell reached over and took her hand, clasping it warmly in his.

"You're much too far away," he sighed. "Remind me not to buy another car with bucket seats."

Andrea bit at the side of her lip to stop the poignant sob from escaping. "I'll remember," she agreed with pseudo brightness.

"My mother called me before we left tonight about a directors' meeting that had been changed."

"You ... you don't have to leave sooner, do you?" She held her breath.

"Mother wanted me to come back tomorrow so I could be prepared for the new Wednesday meeting, but I told her that it was out of the question." There was a sliding smile in her direction before he returned his attention to the road. "She wanted to know if you were very beautiful. Of course, I quickly corrected that statement." The dimpling clefts in his cheek deepened with concealed amusement.

"Thanks a lot," Andrea said, laughing, a warm glow spreading through her once more.

"I told her you were the most beautiful woman in the world," Tell informed her in a frighteningly serious voice.

"Tell!" she whispered, stunned by the vibrancy of his statement.

"Are you going to argue with me?" His challenge was issued in a laughing voice.

"I wouldn't dream of it," she said, her voice trembling.

A car came sweeping around the bend in front of them, taking the curve too wide and forcing Tell onto the shoulder to avoid being sideswiped. The snowplows had mounded the snow on the sides of the road. For several yards their car skimmed the side of the snowbanks before the rear tires hit a soft patch and they were stuck.

"Are you all right?" His mouth was forbiddingly grim and anger burned in his eyes.

"I'm fine," Andrea breathed, a weak smile of reassurance curving her full mouth.

Tell nodded thankfully and shifted the car into gear again, but the rear wheels spun uselessly, unable to get any traction in the snow. A hard smile lifted one corner of his mouth.

"Thanks to that imbecilic driver we seem to be stuck in the snow!" he snapped, slipping the gear into neutral and reaching for his door handle.

"I wouldn't mind being stuck in a snowbank with you forever." What had been meant as a flippant remark came out as a throbbing pledge of love.

The dark head jerked around toward her. "You picked a damned awkward time to say something like that," Tell muttered savagely, but despite the harshness of his low voice, she knew it was without anger.

He seemed to release her gaze reluctantly as he opened the car door, cold mountain air rushing in before the door was slammed shut. The rear trunk was opened, followed shortly by sounds of a shovel digging away the snow near the rear tires. The trunk lid was closed and Tell was sliding behind the wheel again. After rocking back and forth a few times, the tires found a grip and the car pulled onto the road.

CHAPTER THREE

SEVERAL MILES from the spot where they had been forced off the road, Tell turned the car into a side road and switched off the engine. Andrea's heart was doing somersaults as she watched him remove his winter coat and toss it into the back seat. With deliberation marking his movements, he turned in the seat towards her and began slowly unbuttoning her winter coat. In a few seconds, her coat had joined his in the rear seat.

Andrea didn't resist the pressure of his hands burning through the black chiffon sleeves of her dress as he pulled her across his lap and cradled her against his chest. The fingers of one hand lightly caressed her cheek.

"Now, tell me again what you said earlier," he commanded arrogantly.

"I said," she whispered lovingly, "that I would willingly be stuck in a snowbank with you forever."

Kissing first the corner of her eye, then her nose and cheek, he finally reached her lips. "Now, tell me what you really meant by that," he ordered.

"Darling," Andrea moaned softly, pressing her throbbing mouth against the resistance of his. Still he refused to let her feel the fire of his kiss.

"Say it," he growled huskily. "I have to know that you love me as much as I love you."

Breathing in sharply, she was no longer afraid to put her feelings into words. "I love you, Tell. I love you."

His mouth closed fiercely possessive over hers. It was a kiss more wild and glorious than any they had ever shared. The blood pounded through her veins with the wonder of it. His hands were roughly caressing her, crushing her against him, unaware of the strength he was using, and Andrea was oblivious to the pain of her bruised flesh. With a supreme effort, Tell dragged his mouth away from hers, his lean fingers burying her face against his chest, his heart pounding, his breathing ragged and uneven.

"The first time I saw you registering at the desk, I thought you were a beautiful woman and nothing more," he muttered against the silken curtain of her hair. "When you were there at the restaurant, I thought you'd followed me to attract my attention. The desk clerk had made my reservation and it would have been easy for you to bribe him to find out where I would be. I asked you to dine with me only to find out what other tricks you would use. Each time I led the conversation down a personal channel, you shied away and I began to doubt for the first time. When I suddenly realized that it was another man who had made you so wary, a black rage swept over me. I convinced myself it was self-pity and you would get over the hurt in time."

"I was over it." Her hands caressed the strong column of his neck. "I was simply afraid."

"I didn't intend to seek you out again," he sighed. "Then I saw you coming down Bailey's Beach. You were so graceful, like a gazelle," a hand ran caressingly down the length of her thigh, "with those long, shapely legs and that fawn-colored hair and large hazel eyes. I don't know if it was the white backdrop of snow or what, but I suddenly pictured you against white sheets lying naked in my arms. I never wanted any woman as much as I wanted you at that moment. Coldly, I decided to seduce you. Once I had possessed you, I was certain the physical attraction would fade just as it had done all the other times."

"But you didn't." Andrea frowned into his shirt collar. The hand holding the back of her head refused to let her draw away from his chest to look into his face.

He burned a kiss against her temple. "I didn't, but I had it all planned. Then Chris showed up at the bar and everything went wrong from there. I've never been jealous in my life, but if he'd touched you, however innocently, I would have gladly bashed his handsome Adonis face in."

"Was he handsome?" She smiled and nuzzled his throat.

"You know damned well he was," Tell said, laughing, lifting his head to gaze into her face, soft and radiant with her love. "I still don't know why I let you say 'no' to me that night. I knew I could have persuaded you to change your mind, but I didn't try. Maybe because I wanted it to mean as much to you as it would to me. I think that's when I silently admitted that there was a very good possibility that I was falling in love with you. Andrea—" his expression grew serious "—in the past,

I've thought I was on the brink of loving a woman and I've made love to many, but I've never told anyone that I loved them. You do believe me, don't you?"

"I believe you," she murmured with a throbbing ache. "But I wouldn't have cared if you'd loved a hundred women before me as long as you love me now."

"Andrea? It means a dream called woman," he said huskily. "That's what you are to me, a heavenly dream that I'd given up hope of ever coming true."

"Darling," her voice caught on a sob, "I love you more than my life—and I never thought I'd ever be able to say that again."

"What a fool that man was to leave you for someone else," he spoke against her lips. "But I'm glad he was a fool."

"I can't compare what I felt for Dale with the way I feel for you, Tell," Andrea declared throatily. "I was a girl and I loved a boy. Now I'm a woman and I love a man. I love—"

His mouth absorbed the rest of her words, bringing an end to the talking. Her lips parted readily under his passionately exploring kiss, and rippling muscles beneath his dark evening suit crushed and molded her ever closer to the hardness of his body. The flames of desire that raged through her veins were an awesome and splendored thing; pagan and primitive, yet seeming to be blessed by some heavenly deity.

The expertise and mastery of his touch made the impact of the experience all the more shattering. Love made the hunger for each other insatiable as they strained at the physical restrictions that kept them apart. His tie had been torn off and the collar of his shirt opened. Beneath her hands, his naked chest burned from the heat radiating within and the hammer of his heartbeat pounded against her fingers.

"I want you," Tell muttered thickly, bruising her lips.

Andrea shuddered. "Yes." The answer was an acknowledgement of his need and her own.

"You're trembling." The low pitch of his voice vibrated over her, increasing the tremors.

"I'm afraid," she breathed shakily.

His dark head raised a fraction of an inch, a frown knitting his smooth forehead. "Of me?" he questioned in mocking disbelief.

"I've never been with a man before. I don't want to disappoint you, Tell."

The contents of her whispered statement took a few seconds to sink in. When it did, he became rigidly still, then his fingers curled into the tender flesh of her upper arm and she was lifted and pushed roughly out of his embrace.

"Tell, I love you." She reached out hesitantly to touch him, balanced and swaying toward him in the passenger seat.

The knuckles of his brown fingers were turning white as he gripped the steering wheel, head bowed. "I know." He breathed in deeply. "I love you and I want you. But not in a car. Not for you. It's too sordid and .... Just stay there," he ordered crisply, holding up a warning hand as she leaned towards him.

The harshly forbidding set of his features kept Andrea in her seat, a glow of happiness shining through her own throbbing need that his concern was first for her pleasure and not his own. The incredible love in her heart let not one word of persuasion pass from her lips as Tell started the car and returned to the main road. The silence during the rest of the drive to the lodge was emotionally charged and razor-thin, yet infinitely satisfying because of its cause.

When Tell unlocked the door to her room, his fingers closed over the key for an instant. Then he suddenly handed it to her. Tense, slightly trembling masculine fingers touched her cheek as Andrea stared at him.

Leaning down, he lightly brushed her lips. "Good night, my love." Then he was striding down the hall away from her.

In a dreamlike state, Andrea changed into her nightclothes. She was filled with the rapturous blessing of shared love and had never felt more loved and wanted in her life. And Tell loved her with and unselfishness that she had not believed a man was capable of feeling. It made him all the more precious to her.

When her head touched the pillow, an ugly voice jeered, "You didn't tell him. How much is he going to love you when he finds out the truth about you?"

"I'll tell him in the morning," Andrea whispered her promise aloud. "He loves me. He'll understand, I know he will. We love each other too much. It can't be any other way."

The security of knowing she possessed his love

wrapped warm arms about Andrea. The peace and contentment she had in her sleep had not been experienced in a very long time. It was late mid-morning before she finally opened her eyes. The heady memory of the night before made her hug her arms around her to keep the wild joy from bursting her heart.

Since Tell hadn't called, Andrea decided he was probably waiting in the lobby for her, thoughtfully letting her sleep late. Laying out a tan sweater with an olive leaf design and a pair of matching olive green slacks on the bed, she quickly stepped under the stinging shower spray to wash the grains of sleep from her face. After the hurried shower, she pulled on a short terry-cloth robe, forsaking her regular makeup in favor of moisturizing cream, a little eyeshadow and lipstick.

Running a quick brush over her windblown hairstyle, she noticed the ends of her dark blond hair were tipped with gold from the hours spent in the snow and the sun. It was a nice effect, she decided, and wondered if Tell liked it. The knock on the door sent her floating to answer it. Her heart was already saying that Tell was on the other side.

"Good morning." He was leaning against the door frame, his dark eyes raking her from head to bare toe.

"Good morning," she answered breathlessly.

Then Tell was laughing softly, stepping into the room, closing the door behind him and sweeping her into his arms. With hard, demanding kisses he again staked his ownership of her love and she acknowledged his claim readily.

47

"You shouldn't have let me sleep late," she protested.

Her senses were filled with the intoxicating aroma from his smoothly shaven cheeks and the heady scent of his maleness.

"I had a lot of very important things to do." His mouth explored the hollow of her throat, sending tingles down her spine where his hands were roughly carressing her back and hips. "And—" he breathed in deeply, dragging his hands from their arousing task to close over her wrists, which were wound tightly around his neck. He pulled them away and forced Andrea to stand free. "If you don't stop trying to seduce me, I'll forget why I came here."

"You didn't come to see me?" Andrea teased.

"I didn't intend to see so much of you." His mocking gaze danced pointedly over the short terry robe and the long length of her legs that it exposed. "Go get some clothes on while I can still think rationally and I'll tell you what we're going to do."

Andrea started for her bedroom loft, pausing near the stairs to smile back at him. "What are we going to do?" she asked. "I mean, I have a sweater and slacks laid out that I intended to wear, but ...."

"Just get some clothes on." His smile thinned slightly as a dark fire leaped into his gaze. "And when you're finished with that, you can start packing."

"Packing?" she repeated, turning all the way around to face him, her back to the stairs.

"Yes, packing," Tell answered, walking to her almost

48

with reluctance. He placed his hands lightly on her shoulders as if to ensure that a safe distance was maintained between them. "We're driving back to San Francisco as soon as you're ready. I want you to meet my family and my friends. Mother has invited you to stay with us, so it's all arranged."

"Tell—" Andrea began.

"I don't want you out of my sight," he interrupted firmly. "I wouldn't be able to stand having you in Oregon while I was in San Francisco." He turned her around and pointed her towards the stairs. "Now go and get packing."

"Wait." She resisted his efforts, taking two steps up the stairs before pivoting again. "First there's something I have to tell you."

"Whatever it is—" he shook his dark head patiently "—can wait until we're on our way. It's three hours more or less to drive. We can do plenty of talking on the way."

"No." Andrea was insistent. She would not put off telling him the truth any longer. "I have to explain to you before we go. I should have told you before. I meant to, but—"

"If it's waited this long, it can wait a little longer."

"No, it can't wait. The longer I put it off, the harder it will be to explain so you'll understand."

"Andrea." His patience was thinning. The ring of the telephone pierced the room, and he pivoted sharply toward it. "I'll answer that while you get ready," he stated crisply. "If it's your employer, I'll explain that you're quitting and won't be back."

49

For a paralyzed instant, Andrea was incapable of reaction; cold fear freezing her legs. When she did race for the telephone, those frozen seconds allowed Tell to reach it first.

"Tell, no!" she cried as he picked up the receiver. "Give me the phone, please!"

His hand covered the mouthpiece. "Go and get dressed and start packing," he ordered, then removed his hand from the receiver. "Hello."

Biting into her lip, she could barely hear the male voice responding on the other end of the wire. It was John, of course. She knew it even though she could hardly hear the voice well enough to recognize it. He was the only one who would call her. It was too late wishing that she had phoned him yesterday. Her frightened gaze became fixed on Tell's face.

"Yes," he said in answer to a question put to him by the caller. "Who's calling, please?"

There was a fraction of a second's pause before his gaze, darkening to black, swung slowly to Andrea, piercingly intent and terrifyingly cold. His lean, handsome features turned to impenetrable granite as he held the receiver to her.

"It's your husband." His statement seethed with icy, satirical arrogance.

Her hand clutched the opening of her robe, trying to check the nausea rising within. Despair clouded her eyes as her trembling fingers accepted the receiver. Her lashes fluttered tightly down when Tell spun away, rigid strides carrying him to the window of her room.

Twice Andrea opened her mouth before any sound came out. "Hello."

"Andrea? Is that you? Are you all right?" John's anxious puzzled voice answered her immediately.

"Yes, yes, I'm fine," she responded, wishing the floor would open and swallow her up.

"I phoned yesterday and left a message. When you didn't call I became worried."

"I ... I was out ... most of the day," she faltered. Her tongue nervously moistened her lips; her tear-filled gaze turned toward the ceiling as she tried to breathe through the pain in her chest. "It was too late to phone when I cam in last night."

"You were out last night?" he repeated.

"Yes."

"With the ... uh ... man who answered the phone?"

"Yes." Her voice broke. She closed her eyes tightly. A tear slipped from her lashes and she roughly brushed it from her cheek.

There was hesitation on the other end before John spoke. "Did you ... Andrea, did you tell him about me yet?"

"No," Andrea swallowed.

"Oh, Andrea," John sighed heavily. "What have you done to yourself this time?"

"I don't know." A brittle, soft laugh accompanied her words. It was either that or cry.

"It's my fault. It's all my fault," he murmured.

"Don't.... don't say that," she protested.

John breathed in deeply. "Call me ... when you can.

I'm sorry, Andie, I didn't mean to spoil anything ...."

"Yes, I am, too. Goodbye."

A deadly quiet filled the room after the receiver clicked on the hook. Cowardly wishing she could run rather than face Tell's coldly accusing eyes, Andrea slowly turned to the rigidly erect figure staring out of the window. There was no sound but the beating of her heart.

The distance between them was more than just physical, but her hesitant steps tried to bridge it. The outline of his tightly clenched jaw stopped her a foot or so behind him.

"That's what I wanted to explain to you, Tell," she began nervously. "I ... I know it was a terrible shock for you to find out that way and I know I deceived you by not telling you the truth before, but, Tell, I was going to. I know how it must look, but ... " Her voice cracked with a checked sob. "Darling, I love you," she pleaded for his understanding. "I love you."

He whirled around, the flat of his hand slashing across her cheek. The force of it sent her reeling backward, the impetus stopped by the hands that reached out to catch her. Remorse flashed instantly across his face before it again became sternly harsh and forbidding. Tell immediately jerked his hands from her shoulders.

"What a fool I am!" he muttered savagely.

Automatically, her hand had covered the smarting pain of her cheek. Now Andrea drew it away, her chin lifting with faint proudness.

"I was the fool, Tell, not you," she said softly but

firmly. "All I can do now is ask that you let me explain."

His eyes bored into her and she met them unflinchingly. "Answer me this," Tell commanded arrogantly, "was that man on the phone your husband or not?"

"I am legally married to him," Andrea admitted, "but . . . ."

"Are you separated?"

"Tell, please!" Hopelessly, she tried to stop his questions so she could explain in her own way.

"Are you separated?" he repeated forcefully, black fury blazing in his eyes, letting her see that his temper was held by a very thin thread.

"No!" she acknowledged in frustration.

"And I don't suppose you love him," Tell jeered.

"I'm very fond of him." Nervously she ran her fingers through the sides of her hair. "But I never have actually loved him."

"Then why did you marry him? Is he rich?"

"That's beside the point," Andrea protested helplessly.

"I take it that means 'yes,' doesn't it?" His mouth curved into a bitter cynical line. "Now I understand what you meant when you said you'd never known a man. How could I have been so naïve as to think you were trying to explain that you were a virgin? You were really saying that you had a mouse for a husband, weren't you?"

"Stop it!" she cried. "You don't know what you're saying!"

"Don't !?" Tell sneered. "Only a henpecked husband would let his wife come to a resort by herself. He had to know that every red-blooded male that saw you would make some kind of advance."

"Stop it, Tell!" She placed her hands over her ears to deafen the flow of his sarcasm.

Her left wrist was viciously jerked away. "And don't try to make me believe that you didn't intend to accept some of those advances!" he growled, twisting her hand in front of her face. "You're not even wearing a wedding ring. When did you take it off? After you left his house?"

A sob rasped her throat. "It's being repaired. I lost one of the stones. I swear, it's in the jewelry shop!"

"You disgust me!" Anger vibrated through his huskily controlled voice as he abruptly released her wrist.

"Please. Give me a chance to explain." Her chin quivered uncontrollably.

"It wouldn't make any difference," he said coldly. "If you were divorced and free to marry, I would never want you for my wife. If you could so conveniently forget one husband, you could do the same with me."

"No."

"Here." He reached into his pocket and removed a ring box. "I bought this for you. You might as well have it. It's memento, a trophy"— he added sarcastically— "to show that your hunt wasn't totally unsuccessful."

The lid of the tiny box flipped open as he crushed it into her hand. The rainbow colors of a large diamond solitaire laughed mockingly at her. Andrea closed her eyes against the reflecting brilliance of the exquisitely simple and expensive ring. Weakly, she tried to hand it back to him.

"Keep it, I said!" Tell snapped.

Then his long strides were carrying him to the door. On trembling legs, she hurried after him, grabbing the door before he could close it behind him.

"Please, give me a chance to explain," she pleaded.

"Accept that it's over, Andrea. Nothing you can say is going to change that." A cold smile was carved into the bronze mask. "Maybe you'll have better luck with your next sucker."

The door was yanked free of her hold and slammed shut.

"Tell!" Her fingers closed over the knob, but she didn't attempt to open the door. Sobbing heavily, she leaned against the door, trying to wash away the intense pain with tears.

Long minutes went by before Andrea regained any degree of control. He had made it very clear that he didn't want to listen to her, but she loved him too desperately not to try again. Somehow, she had to make him understand. Scrubbing the tears from her cheeks, she forced her faltering legs to carry her to the telephone. After taking deep breaths to steady her voice, she contacted the desk.

"Mr. Stafford's room, please," she requested.

"I'm sorry, Mr. Stafford isn't in," the clerk replied.

"Do ... do you know where he is?" She faltered for a

second as a knife of despair was plunged into her heart.

"He stopped by the desk a few minutes ago, miss, and asked us to prepare his bill, then he went out."

"I see." She swallowed tightly. "Thank you."

Hanging up the telephone, she realized that Tell had probably guessed she would try again to explain and had deliberately not returned to his room. He probably also had guessed that she would not want to make a scene in the lobby or any other public place. That left only one alternative.

With shaking fingers, she withdrew the lodge stationery from the drawer of a small table. Quickly, she began writing the things that she hadn't been given the chance to tell him. Time was critical if she wanted to be sure he received her note before he left, but Andrea was careful not to leave anything out in her haste.

A frightening amount of time passed before the letter was completed and sealed in an envelope. Racing up the stairs to the bedroom loft, she dressed swiftly and dashed back down the steps and out the door, the precious envelope clutched tightly in her hand.

Short of the lobby, Andrea slowed her pace, dredging deep in her reserves for some measure of poise before approaching the desk. Unconsciously, she held her breath as she walked in, her eyes automatically searching for Tell. He wasn't among the people in the lobby, which meant he had either not returned or had already left the resort. With fingers crossed, she walked to the front desk.

"Has Mr. Stafford checked out yet?" The brightness

of her simple question sounded unnaturally brittle.

"Not yet, miss," was the reply.

With false nonchalance, she placed the envelope on the desk counter, the face bearing Tell's name turned toward the clerk. "When he does, would you see that he gets this note?"

"Be glad to," the man nodded.

The smile on his face indicated that he guessed it was a love letter. He wasn't too far wrong, Andrea thought to herself as she turned away. It did contain her heart. It was all there, unprotected and exposed for Tell's examination.

Leaving the lobby, Andrea didn't return to her room, but found a strategic spot where she could watch the people in the lobby without being seen. The anxiety of waiting was nearly unbearable: her legs shaking, her hands clasped unknowingly in prayer. When the tension had built to a screaming pitch, Tell's familiar lean figure walked through the outer doors toward the front desk.

Hardly daring to breathe, Andrea watched him check out. Fear trembled through her that the clerk would forget her note, but at the very last moment, he handed it to him. The polite smile faded from Tell's face, changing his facade into lines of uncompromising hardness, which were too severe to be handsome.

She waited; waited for the moment when he would open the envelope and read her note, waited for that instant when the light of understanding would melt the coldness of his expression. Then, she would let herself be seen.

57

None of that happened. Instead, he tore it in two. With freezing indifference on his face, he tore those pieces into halves again and discarded them all in a wastebasket.

Her hand automatically checked the cry of pain that bubbled to her lips. Tears streamed down her cheeks as she stumbled down the hall to her room. She had handed Tell her heart and he had torn it into pieces and thrown it away. Drowning her pillow with tears, Andrea cried long and hard until only dry, heaving sobs racked her body. Finally, even those stopped.

Leaden feet carried her hollow shell down the loft steps to the telephone. Staring sightlessly into space, she waited for the front desk to answer.

"This is Andrea Grant." The identification was made in a hoarse voice. "I would like you to call the airport and make arrangements for me for a chartered flight to Medford, Oregon, this afternoon, and then have my bill drawn up."

"Certainly. We'll take care of it right away, Miss Grant."

"It's Mrs. Grant," she corrected coldly. "Mrs. John Grant."

"Yes, Mrs. Grant," the puzzled voice on the other end acknowledged.

CHAPTER FOUR

"SET THE LUGGAGE inside the door," Andrea instructed, replacing the housekey in her purse and extracting the taxi fare to hand to the driver.

"Thank you, miss."

Hestitating, Andrea let her gaze sweep over the familiar, large white structure with its mock tower on one side. Home. But home is where the heart is, she thought bitterly, and her heart wasn't here. Inhaling deeply, she reminded herself that she was the only one to blame for that. If she had been honest with Tell in the beginning, he might have understood. At least her heart wouldn't have been torn into pieces and thrown away.

The agony was to go on living and breathing ... and remembering.

The sound of the taxi pulling out of the driveway into the rural countryside made her aware that she was still standing outside the door in the brisk December air. A shake of her head chased the torment from her hazel eyes. There was still yet another gauntlet to face, a loving one, but one that she had to endure without faltering just the same.

She pushed open the front door and stepped on to the figured rug that protected the hardwood floor. Large, antique hanging lamps, converted now from gas to electricity, lighted the foyer. Mrs. Davison, the housekeeper, appeared at the entrance of the hallway leading to the kitchen, hastily wiping floured hands on her apron. Her mouth opened in astonishment at the sight of Andrea, before the thin face changed into a smile.

"Andrea, we didn't expect you back until the end of the week," she announced, bustling forward. "Not that I can say that I'm not glad you're back, because I am. Why didn't you let us know you were coming today? Frank could have met you at the airport instead of your paying a taxi to come all this way. Mr. Grant has been brooding all day. He didn't touch a speck of lunch, and I'd fixed a really nice steelhead trout, too. Here, let me take your coat."

Slipping it from her shoulders, Andrea handed it to the housekeeper. "Where is John now, Mrs. Davison?"

The older woman pursed her lips together in disapproval. "Sitting in his study staring at the fire just like he's been doing ever since that attorney, Frank Graham, left."

"I'll let him know I'm back," Andrea said quietly.

The housekeeper cocked her head to one side in a listening attitude. "I don't think you'll need to."

At almost the same moment, Andrea heard the galloping sound. She had a half a second to brace herself before an Irish setter came careening around the corner and launched himself at her. He danced madly around her, winding around her legs and shoving his flame gold head against her hands, only to be overcome by joy and spin wildly away, whining his ecstatic happiness at her return.

"Settle down, Shawn," a male voice admonished the dog gently.

The setter dashed toward his master, circling the wheelchair to sit on the left side, a quivering mass of excitement. Wherever Shawn was, Andrea knew John would not be far. The two were inseparable. The only times the setter left his side were when she took him for an exercising walk.

"Andie." A faint smile tenderly lifted his mouth as John greeted her, his warm gray eyes examining the tautness of her answering smile and the sharp edges of partially concealed pain in her eyes.

"Hello, John." She walked quickly to his side before he could see too much, lightly clasping his hands and bending to brush his cheek with an affectionate kiss.

"Got tired of all that skiing, did you?" Both of them knew the comment was made for the housekeeper's benefit.

"Something like that," Andrea said, nodding.

"Fix us some cocoa, Mrs. Davison, and bring it into the study for us." John's orders always sounded like a request, but he expected them to be obeyed just the same.

Releasing her hands, he flicked the lever to turn his wheelchair around, the quiet motor providing the power to operate the chair without anyone's assistance. The wheelchair gave him the mobility that a logging accident had deprived him of and the independence that was so much a part of him. Andrea followed him quietly.

Flames licked greedily over partially burned logs, their

61

yellow tongues outlined by the hearth blackened with many years of use. Tan stone blended with the richly paneled walls and the leather-bound books on the shelves. The furniture, mostly antique and all of it old, had been in the room for years adding to the comfortable atmosphere.

Despite the early evening hour, the firelight was the only source of light, flickering on the smooth walls. The dimness of the study increased its air of cocoon comfort.

Andrea walked past the large, leather wing chair and ottoman sitting to the side of the fireplace, and proceeded instead to stand on the brick area directly in front of the fire. Pretending to ward off an imaginary chill, she held out her hands to the flame.

"Well, did you break anything while you were on your holiday?" John asked lightly, rolling his wheelchair to a stop on the alpaca rug.

The offer to accept part of her pain had been made. Without turning around, Andrea pictured the man who had made it: his strong, gentle face, distinguished and handsome, wearing his fifty-plus years lightly; the broad shoulders and powerful arms, and the paralysis from the waist down that kept him confined to that wheelchair. Never had she heard him complain or express self-pity.

For more than three years she had accepted every offer of help John made, transferring her pain, her grief, her heartache on to his shoulders. The desire was intense to do it again, to pour out her heartbreak and love for Tell. But she was an adult. It was time she stopped using him as a crutch and began to accept the responsibility and the results of all the things that she said and did.

Taking a deep breath, she glanced over her shoulder, tossing her dark blond hair slightly in a deliberately careless gesture and smiling ruefully. "I came out with a few bruises, but nothing that won't heal in time," she lied.

"Are you sure, Andrea?" he asked in a doubting voice.

A large lump stuck in her throat, tears burning the back of her eyes. "I never said that the bruises didn't hurt, John," she said tightly.

Nervously, she turned away from the fire and walked to the smoke stand between the wing chair and John. Carefully, she filled and packed tobacco in his favorite pipe the way he had taught her, and carried it to him, lighting it as he drew on it slowly. Blinking to keep the tears at bay, she knelt on the floor, curling her legs on the alpaca rug and leaning against him. The aroma of the pipe tobacco blended pleasantly with the fragrant scent of burning pipe.

"It was only a holiday thing," Andrea stared into the fire. "A shipboard romance on skis," she added with wry flippancy.

"And it came to an abrupt end when I called," he sighed. "My first thought when your friend answered the phone was that he was a doctor and you'd been injured. I suppose that's why I was so hasty in claiming my relationship. Was he very angry when he found out?"

"I suppose so," she hedged. Her cheek rubbed the woolen, plaid coverlet on his legs, the same cheek that had felt the sting of Tell's hand, that hadn't inflicted nearly the pain that his harshly bitter words had carried.

"Why didn't you tell him, Andie?

"I didn't want him to get the wrong impression," she sighed this time. "You know what I mean, John—that I was a married woman looking for an affair. I thought he would be good company and fun. He was."

His large hand began to gently stroke her hair. "It's my fault, Andie. When I suggested you marry me, it was with the best of intentions. I was older. I should have known better."

"You're forgetting the vicious rumors that went around when I moved into this house after daddy died and Dale and I broke up." She grimaced in memory.

"Rather flattering they were to me, considering my circumstances," John said dryly, "but so cruelly damaging for a young girl like you. Let's not forget my mercenary relatives."

"Oh, John, it was never your money." Wistfully she turned, laying her head back against his leg and gazing up at him. "I needed your strength and your comfort and, in a way, you needed me."

"You always need the affection of the people you care about," he smiled in reassurance. "Still, I should have found some other way than marriage. There are some people who would question the truth of our motives. You've been exposed to so much pain in such a short time, I would never forgive myself if our arrangement stood in the way of your happiness."

"John, please, don't be blaming yourself." There was no way now that Andrea could ever confide in him that

64

his worst fear had come true. "If a man really loves me, he'll understand. And if he doesn't—" her voice cracked with pain "—then he isn't really the one who can make me happy, is he?"

The words sounded very wise and profound, yet Andrea couldn't truly believe them. She did love Tell and he could have made her happy, very happy.

"Andie—" A tap on the study door stopped him.

The brass knob turned and the housekeeper walked in, carrying a tray with two mugs of cocoa and a plate of sugar cookies. Their scent had the Irish setter dancing a jig behind the housekeeper. Andrea rose to her feet to take the tray. Mrs. Davison's brief appearance ended the mood of intimacy, and John didn't attempt to bring about its return.

THE MATING CALL of a bird trilled through the window, but Andrea's pounding head didn't appreciate its song. Rolling onto her side, she pulled the sheets up to cover her ears, but the bright notes couldn't be blocked out. The breeze carried the fragrant scent of pear blossoms. Through closed eyes, she could still see the light of the morning sun.

Moaning a protest, she reverted to her former position on her back, pressing a hand to her forehead behind which a dull ache pounded. Her eyelids felt weighted with lead. Tiredness yawned in every muscle.

"Why do I take those sleeping pills?" Andrea murmured thickly.

The answer was obvious. There had been too many

sleepless nights without them, and too many nights when exhausted sleep had been punctuated by torturous dreams of Tell. Almost six months had passed, and his image was as vividly sharp as her memories of the brief time they had spent together.

Looking back, Andrea knew she had never really fooled John when she had tried to convince him that first night home that she hadn't fallen in love. Perhaps she had for a short time, but her actions had given away the true state of her feelings. He seemed to respect the fact that she wanted to get through this on her own and made no attempt to encourage a confidence that she was reluctant to give.

When Dale had deserted her, the pain had eased to a dull ache within a few short weeks. This time, the hurt was as tormentingly real as it was that morning Tell had hurled his sarcastic rejection at her. Aching misery was her constant companion, hiding not very successfully in the haunted recesses of her eyes.

Raking her fingernails through her hair and lifting the dark blond strands away from her face, Andrea glanced wearily toward the gold antique clock on her night table. Blinking, she looked at it again, unable to believe that the hands could actually be saying it was eleven.

"Oh, no!" she groaned, throwing back the covers and sliding quickly out of the brass bed.

With tired haste, she stumbled to the bathroom, and splashed cold water on her sleep-drugged face. A lethargy that couldn't be washed away slowed her movements despite her attempts to hurry. Ignoring the time-consuming task of applying makeup, Andrea settled for a quick brush through her hair and a touch of lipstick, then pulled on a pair of denim jeans and a sleeveless top.

The effects of the sleeping pill were still dulling her senses as her barely coordinated reflexes directed her down the stairs. Without pausing, she turned down the corridor leading to the kitchen. Mrs. Davison was standing at the sink rinsing a head of lettuce when Andrea entered the room.

Glancing at the clock above her head, the housekeeper said dryly, "You made it up in time for me to still say good morning."

"Why did you let me sleep so late?" Andrea frowned, obeying the hand that waved her into a chair at the oak table. "I was going to help you get the rooms ready."

"Mr. Grant said for me to let you sleep as late as possible." Wiping her hands on her apron, the woman walked to the refrigerator, poured out a glass of orange juice and set it on the table in front of Andrea. A few seconds later it was followed by a cup of coffee and doughnuts. "And the rooms are all ready, so you needn't be worrying about that."

"I would still liked to have helped." The juice helped wash the cottony taste from her mouth. "I didn't want to sleep this late."

"It seems to me you should be blaming those sleeping pills for that." Mrs. Davison sniffed her disapproval. "A girl your age shouldn't be taking them."

Andrea wrapped her hands around the coffee cup. "The doctor prescribed them for me."

"Those pills may help you sleep, but they don't cure the cause of your not sleeping," the housekeeper observed caustically. "It seems to me the doctor should have recognized it."

"I ... " Andrea started to protest, then closed her mouth. There was no point in debating the issue. "What time are Mrs. Collins and her daughter supposed to arrive?"

"This afternoon some time. Mr. Grant told me to plan to have dinner for them, but not lunch. He isn't sure if her husband's coming or not, but I have a room ready just in case. You've met Mrs. Collins before, haven't you?"

"Yes, a year ago. No, two years ago it was," Andrea corrected tiredly. "She seemed very nice."

"Oh, there's no doubt, she's a real lady," Mrs. Davison assured her. "She used to spend a couple of weeks here every summer, her and her husband, but that was when her daughter was wearing braces. Once they came off, her visits were less frequent and shorter. Mr. Grant is her daughter's godfather, but I imagine he told you that."

"Yes."

"The last ime I saw her, she was such a pretty little thing, so happy and full of life, and kind like her mother," the housekeeper sighed, shaking the water from the lettuce and placing it on the drainboard. "It's hard to believe that little Nancy is twenty years old and engaged. Oh, it'll be good to see her again."

"Yes," Andrea agreed automatically. She hadn't met

68

the girl before, but she remembered Mrs. Collins showing pictures of her daughter.

"It'll be good to have visitors staying in the house again." The iron-gray head gave an aggressively affirmative nod. "These past months since Christmas, this place has seemed like a mausoleum."

The pallor in Andrea's cheeks intensified. Her cloud of depression had seemed to darken everyone's spirits. She had already guessed that John's invitation to Mrs. Collins had been issued in the hopes of channeling Andrea's attention away from her misery and heartache, and providing a distraction to ease the pain. His thoughtfulness touched her, but Andrea doubted that his plan would have any lasting success.

Finishing one of the doughnuts, she pushed the saucer with the other aside and drained the last of the coffee from her cup. She fixed a bright smile on her face, one that her jangled nerves couldn't endorse, and turned to the housekeeper.

"Can I help you with lunch?" she inquired.

"The casserole is in the oven and everything else is done except this salad," Mrs. Davison replied. "You could cut some flowers from the garden. It'd be nice to have a few spring bouquets scattered about the house."

It was not the kind of task that Andrea had in mind. This was one of those times when she didn't particularly want to be alone with her thoughts, although there were times when she had to be alone. But she had offered to help, and Mrs. Davison had made a suggestion. There was little else she could do but agree.

69

With an acquiescing nod, Andrea left the house by the rear door, stopping at the small utility shed to collect the garden shears, a small oblong wicker basket and a pair of cotton gloves. Ignoring the dull throb of her head, she vowed to concentrate on her task.

Through the irises, the late tulips, the daisies and the roses, she succeeded. The route of her snipping had taken her to the white board fence separating the house grounds from the orchard. The pear trees were heavy with blossoms, their scent faintly perfuming the May air.

May and December. Once, the coupling of those two months would have reminded her of the snide comments made about her marriage to John. Now, she could only consider that the heartbreak she had felt in December was just as agonizing in May.

Leaning on the board fence, she stared at the beautiful white blossoms, a symbol of spring and the rebirth of life. It seemed as if she had only lived those few short days with Tell. Her life before and after was a vacuum.

"It isn't fair," she whispered in self-pity. Surely she had been punished enough.

The haunted, dispirited look filled her eyes, eyes that were too tired to cry—but the tears were shed within. Wrapped in the torment of lost love, Andrea didn't hear the footsteps approaching as she stared sightlessly at the flower-laden trees.

"If it was any other time of year, I would swear you were out here planning to steal some pears," a low voice teased.

Andrea pushed herself away from the fence with a

start. Using a gloved hand to brush a dark gold strand of hair from her face, she concealed her broken look, allowing herself the precious seconds she needed to put on her mask of composure.

"Good morning, Adam," she greeted the sandy-haired man evenly.

"Andrea," he smiled naturally, a winning smile that added to his all-American look. His gaze turned to the trees. "I don't know which part of the season I like best. When the trees are white with blossoms, or the first green pears are loading the branches, or in the fall when gold globes weight the branches."

"It depends which feeling is uppermost in your mind at a particular time," she answered lightly.

"What do you mean?" He slid her a curious glance.

"If you're feeling particularly aesthetic, then the blossom time is the best. The green pear urge is hard to ignore when you're hungry, and you can't ignore the fall greed when you start counting the profits hanging on the trees."

Adam Fitzgerald threw back his head and laughed, "I should have known you would make some remark like that!"

Recently, twisted by the pain that dogged her every footstep, her tongue had become bitterly cynical. ".You work too hard sometimes, Adam. At harvest time, Carolyn hardly ever sees you. She couldn't ... you're always here. And when you aren't here, you're at some logging camp."

"There's a lot of work to be done. John's given me a

71

lot of responsibility. Carolyn understands that," he replied patiently.

"She's much more understanding than I would be," Andrea told him, then sighed ruefully. "I should be saying how grateful I am for the way you take care of everything for John. I know how much he relies on you. Instead, I'm condemning you for doing too much."

"Well—" Adam shrugged "—Carolyn and I will be married next month. In a few years, she'll probably be glad that I'm not around so much."

"Oh, no," Andrea disagreed fervently—a protest that came from her own conviction that if she were married to Tell, she would miss him every minute he was away from her for the rest of her life, regardless of the reason for his absence.

"As long as I'm not gone for very long," he qualified with a mocking smile. "You never did tell me what you were daydreaming about while you were staring at the trees."

"Actually—" Andrea stalled, absently glancing at the basket and the velvet softness of the budding pink rose that touched her hand "—I was thinking that these roses would look nice with a spray of blossoms, and I was wondering if I dared cut one and escape with my life."

"It looks to me as if you already have plenty of flowers in that basket," was his typically male response.

"Mrs. Collins and her daughter are arriving this afternoon. Mrs. Davison thought it would be a good idea to have flowers scattered through the house, and it's a big house."

"I suppose we could spare one small twig of potential pears," Adams surrendered good-naturedly. "Come on, I'll give you a hand."

Holding the flower basket and the shears in one hand, he helped her climb over the fence with the other, then gave them back to her and vaulted over himself. Now that she was committed to adding pear blossoms to her flowers, Andrea decided to pick just the perfect fanning spray to use as a backdrop for the roses.

With Adam following indulgently behind her, she followed the path between the white yard fence and the rows of trees, searching the limbs for the right branch. Several yards farther, she spotted the one she wanted.

"Do you see that small branch where the blossoms fan out, Adam?" She pointed toward it. "Can you reach it?"

"I think so." Taking the shears from her, he stretched his long arms, clasping the branch and snipping it from the tree. "There you are."

"Thank you." She took the spray from him and placed it in the basket with the rest of the flowers.

"Now that I've assured myself that you aren't going to vandalize the orchard, do you suppose we could go to the house?" Adam grinned. "I came to go over the timber leases with John and, I hope, to persuade Mrs. Davidson or someone to invite me to lunch."

"I think that can be arranged," Andrea replied lightly.

Their route along the fence had taken them toward the front of the house. As they turned to cross the fence, they were level with the entrance. This time, Adam

73

agilely vaulted the rails ahead of her, turning as she stepped on to the first board. She reached out to hand him the basket of flowers so her hands could be free to climb the fence. Instead of taking the basket, Adam's hands closed around her waist and lifted her right over the fence.

At the same instant, she realized that a car had stopped in the driveway and doors were being opened and closed. As she made her laughing gasp of protest, Andrea glanced toward the drivway. She stared at the man stepping from the car, the sleeves of his shirt rolled up and the buttons partially unbuttoned to reveal the tanned column of his throat.

It couldn't be! Her mind was playing tricks on her. But the image remained and the man was staring back at her, cold, angry shock in his expression.

It was Tell.

Her gaze swung to the two women climbing out of the opposite side of the car. Andrea wondered what he was doing with Mrs. Collins and her daughter. Was he the fiancé that John had mentioned? Oh, God, she couldn't bear that!

Then she watched his gaze flicker from her face to the man who had swung her to the ground. Not even that morning when he had condemned her so bitterly had she seen his handsome face look as forbidding and coldly arrogant as it did when his black gaze slashed back at her, his nostrils flaring in contempt and disgust.

Andrea knew what Tell was thinking at the moment. He was concluding that she and Adam.... Her stomach turned with a sickening rush as what little color she possessed receded from her face.

"Good lord, Andrea! What's wrong?" Adam demanded earnestly, his hands clutching her shoulders.

"It's ...." She almost said it was Tell, but at that moment Adam had shook her gently, snapping her head from Tell's pinning gaze. "It's Mrs. Collins. They've arrived."

He glanced over his shoulder. Mrs. Collins and her daughter were walking to the front door, neither of them having noticed Andrea and Adam. Tell was following them. Then Adam returned his attention to her.

"There's no reason to be so upset because they're early," he reproved with a gentle smile. "You know Mrs. Davison is a genius in the kitchen. With a wave of her magic wand, she'll make the food stretch from three to six."

"Yes, of course," Andrea agreed shakily. He had released her shoulder and she ran a trembling, perspiring palm down the side of her denim jeans.

"There's another reason, isn't there?" He tilted his sandy head to the side.

"Wh—at?" She clutched the basket handle tighter, wondering how much he had read into her stunned reaction. Adam was not only a hardworking overseer, but he was intelligent, too.

"It's your clothes, isn't it?" He tucked her hand under his arm and turned her toward the house. "You wanted to be wearing something a little more chic than blue jeans when the redoubtable Mrs. Collins arrived,

75

didn't you? Well, don't worry about that. You would be eye-catching in sackcloth, but don't tell Carolyn I told you that," he teased lightly. "I don't want a jealous fiancée on my hands a month before our wedding!"

"She knows better than that. I'm hardly the femme fatale that I'm painted," Andrea replied bitterly, remembering the conclusion that had been in Tell's eyes when he had seen her with Adam.

"Hey, Andrea, this is Adam," he said, frowning. "When have I ever pointed a finger at your marriage? I know the circumstances surrounding it and what led John to propose this type of arrangement. I'm not condemning you for it. I never have."

"I'm sorry." Her mouth moved into a faint, nervous smile of apology. "Sometimes I lose my thick skin and become slightly paranoid."

"Well, hold your head up. There's nothing to be ashamed of."

His gentle, bolstering words were just what she needed as he released her arm and reached around to open the front door. John was in the foyer greeting his guests, the Irish setter grinning happily at his side.

CHAPTER FIVE

ARMORED WITH PRIDE, Andrea walked directly to the wheelchair, taking a position at John's side. She was, after all, his wife and therefore the hostess. Her place was beside him greeting their guests. That one of them was the man she loved couldn't be considered at this time.

"There you are, Andie," John smiled up at her. "Out picking flowers, I see."

"Yes." Her side vision caught Tell's twisted, sardonic look that said it wasn't all she had been doing. Her fragile composure nearly dissolved, her smile cracking for an instant as she turned it toward the two women. She deliberately ignored Tell while she rebuilt her defences. "I wanted to have some spring bouquets set around the house as a way of saying welcome."

"That is thoughtful, Andrea, and the flowers look very beautiful," Mrs. Collins replied.

"You remember Rosemary, don't you, Andie?" John inserted, introducing the woman who had just spoken.

"Of course, I do. It's good to see you again, Mrs. Collins," Andrea acknowledged, switching the flower basket to the other side in order to shake hands.

Rosemary Collins was the same age as John, in her fifties. She had retained her youthful beauty. Her hair was still a dark brown, although a close inspection might detect a few gray hairs. Her eyes were a soft brown and her face relatively unlined and wearing a smile with easy grace. The years had added a few pounds, but she was still matronly slim.

"Please, call me Rosemary," she corrected with friendly warmth, then slipped a hand on the young woman's elbow standing at her side and drew her forward. "This is my daughter, Nancy."

Large, expressive blue eyes studied Andrea curiously from a slender oval face framed by silky fine brown hair. Andrea's smile stiffened slightly as she accepted the girl's hand. She doubted that she could shrug off as paranoia the sensation that Nancy Collins was wondering why she had married a man as old as John.

"Your mother has told me about you. I'm glad I'm finally getting to meet you," was Andrea's polite greeting.

"I've been looking forward to it, too," the girl replied, smiling naturally and with the same kindness as her mother.

As the handclasp of greeting ended, Andrea caught the flash of a diamond solitaire on Nancy's left hand, poignantly reminding her of the one hidden in her dresser drawer. She couldn't say why she had kept it. Perhaps to remind herself of what she had lost—as if she needed any reminder.

John's hand touched her arm and Andrea braced herself for the introduction to Tell. She knew she would never be able to offer sincere congratulations to him on his engagement to Nancy. Wildly she searched her mind for some ambiguous remark that would not make her look like a fool.

"Tell, I don't believe you've met Andrea, either," John began.

But his introduction was abruptly halted by Tell's slicing response. "Yes, I have."

Andrea had been carefully avoiding looking directly at him until it was absolutely necessary, but his words shocked her into staring. Her heart stopped as his piercing gaze slashed her to ribbons.

His hard mouth was lifted at one corner in a mocking curl, deriding the pleading look in her eyes. "Actually," he said lazily, "I saw her when we drove in, picking flowers." He placed cutting emphasis on the last words, before he glanced at John. The sardonic expression was replaced by impassive courtesy. "But we haven't been formally introduced. She is your wife?"

John took hold of her hand. It was a touch of warmth that she desperately needed as cold fear raced through her veins. She looked down with gratitude at his reassurance that she was not alone.

"More than that, Tell. She's my secretary, my companion, my supporter and—"

"Your youth?" Tell's quiet insertion held no sarcasm of mockery, but Andrea knew it was there. Concealed from John, but it was there.

Swallowing nervously, Andrea watched the slight narrowing of John's gray eyes as he silently studied Tell. "That, too, I suppose," he admitted after a long moment. "But let me formally introduce you. Andrea, this is Tell Stafford, Rosemary's son. My wife, Andrea."

Her son? Not Nancy's fiancé? Her knees nearly buckled at the announcement. The different surnames had thrown her. In the unexpectedness of seeing him again, Andrea had forgotten that Tell had told her his mother had married again when he was a child. She hadn't realized the additional agony she had felt picturing him in the young woman's arms until it was suddenly cast away.

The discovery made the beautiful smile she gave him blissfully warm and natural. If anything, his expression hardened under the glow of her look. Her hand had been automatically extended in greeting. He glanced at it pointedly. Instantly, her joyous relief dissipated as she thought for one humiliating moment that he was going to rudely ignore her outstretched hand. Then his lean brown fingers closed over it, releasing her hand almost immediately, almost as if there were contamination in her touch.

"And of course all of you remember Adam Fitzgerald," John continued, allowing a slight pause for Andrea and Tell to acknowledge their introduction before drawing the group's attention to the man standing just inside the door, "my manager and my legs."

As everyone turned to greet Adam, Andrea slipped back to take a less obtrusive position behind John's chair and escape their notice for as long as possible. But Tell noticed her attempt to fade into the background, sarcastically raising one dark brow in mockery. Andrea's gaze fell away from his arrogant contempt.

The respite was brief. Much too soon Andrea was pushed to the foreground when John suggested that she show their guests to their rooms, while he quickly went over the timber leases with Adam before lunch. Hotly aware of Tell's dark eyes boring into her back, she led them up the stairs, wasting little time directing them to their respective rooms.

"How thoughtful of John to give me my old room!" Rosemary exclaimed as Andrea opened the door to the damask bedroom, a name she had attached to the room because of the beautiful, old damask bedspread that covered the antique four-poster bed. "He must have remembered how fond I was of the spectacular view of the mountains from this window." She smiled over her shoulder at Andrea. "And Nancy has her same room, too. It's like coming home."

"We expected your husband might accompany you. That's why the adjoining bedroom is prepared for—" Andrea stumbled, unable to speak Tell's name "—your son. I'm sure Mrs. Davison and I could quickly enough get his old room ready. I'm afraid I don't know which one it is."

It was still difficult for her to accept that Tell had spent any time in the house that was her home.

"He used to have the room on the right where the mock tower is." There was a faraway look in Rosemary Collins's eyes as if she were silently reminiscing about a bygone time. "It's a bit separated from the other bedrooms and he always used to like that. If it wouldn't be too much trouble, I'm sure he would like to stay in it."

Andrea's breathing became shallow and uneven as a warm pink flowed into her cheeks. "I'm sorry, Mrs. Collins," she murmured self-consciously. "That's ... in use. It's, er, my room."

"Your room? I ...." The startled voice stopped, but Andrea completed the thought to herself. Rosemary Collins had probably thought that she shared the master bedroom suite downstairs with John. "It doesn't matter," the woman said and shrugged quickly. "Men are seldom as sentimental about such things as women are."

"So you have the tower room?" Tell's voice came mockingly from the connecting door between the two bedrooms.

"Yes," Andrea breathed, her gaze bouncing away from his. "If you'll excuse me—" the request was made to his mother "—I'll have to get these flowers in some water. Lunch will be in about an hour. Please make yourself at home."

Her dignified retreat carried her to the kitchen. There, her legs nearly dissolved as a long-postponed reaction set in, but she wasn't allowed time to adjust to Tell's arrival and whatever implications it might contain or the unforeseen difficulties that might accompany it.

Mrs. Davison's magic wand required a helping hand, and she deputized Andrea to supply it as she bustled about the kitchen to come up with the last-minute items to supplement the original menu for three to extend it to seven—since Adam had received his hoped-for invitation to join them. When the task was successfully accomplished, Andrea barely had time to slip upstairs to her room and change before lunch was served.

John supervised the seating arrangements, placing his two female guests on either side of him at the head of the table. That left Tell and Adam to sit at Andrea's end of the table. Mrs. Davison chose not to eat with them, insisting that she would rather have her meal by herself after they had lunched when she could eat in peace.

Andrea wished she could have had the same alternative. She would rather have eaten alone than endure Tell's cold indifference to her presence. He pointedly avoided addressing any comment directly to her, cutting her out of his conversation with Adam as if she weren't there. To try to carry on polite conversation with the women at the other end of the table was impossible, so Andrea sat through the meal in uncomfortable silence. It was a silence that no one seemed to notice, except perhaps Tell, who cuttingly enforced it.

Gladly, she insisted at the end of the meal that the others take their coffee on the cobblestoned veranda while she helped Mrs. Davison clear the lunch dishes. She dallied in the kitchen until the housekeeper finally shooed her out. There weren't any more excuses for not joining the others.

But how could she treat Tell as a stranger when her every nerve end screamed with the knowledge of his touch, his kiss, his embrace and the love they had shared so briefly? When Andrea thought of the way it had been, and that they might never kiss again, it seemed like a cruel game of pretense.

For a numbed moment she stood in the corridor, dredging her inner resources for some reserve of courage and stamina. Then she heard male footsteps descending the stairs—firm deliberate movements that had to belong to Tell. A fleeting second later she knew she had to speak to him alone and this was her prime opportunity.

As she reached the end of the corridor, Tell was at the bottom of the open staircase turning toward the continuing hallway that would lead him to the rear of the house and the veranda entrance.

"Tell?" Her unconsciously pleading call halted him and he slowly turned around to face her, his leanly chiseled face aristocratically cold and arrogantly hard.

Now that Andrea had his attention without anyone listening, she didn't know what to say She searched his uncompromising expression for some sign that the months apart might have tempered his attitude with compassion. Nothing indicated that he had yielded any measure of his contempt for her as he nonchalantly placed a cigarette between the sardonic line of his lips and snapped a lighter to it. Still she couldn't speak.

"Did you arrange this little rendezvous, Andrea?" His low-pitched voice was ominously soft.

"I had to talk to you alone," she murmured, trying to accept that this man of stone was the same one who had loved her so passionately. "I heard you coming down the stairs and—"

"Don't pretend naïveté that you don't possess!" he snapped viciously. "You know very well that I'm referring to the invitation that was issued to my mother and the postscript to remind me how long it had been since I accompanied her."

Andrea breathed in sharply at his attack. "Tell, I swear I didn't know who you were. I admit that I knew John had invited your mother, but I didn't know she was your mother. That's the truth."

A cloud of smoke was exhaled between them. "The problem with people who don't make a habit of telling the truth, Andrea, is that others seldom believe them when they do."

"It is true!" she repeated forcefully. "I even thought you were Nancy's fiancé until Mrs. Collins said you were her son."

"I see," Tell mocked. "John knew very well who I was."

"That's what I wanted to talk to you about." Andrea stared at her tightly clasped hands. "I didn't tell him about you."

"John must be more gullible than I thought. How did you explain what I was doing in your room?" he jeered. "Fixing a leaking tap?"

"No, of course not," she sighed heavily. "He knows I met someone, but I never told him your name."

"Naturally, he was very understanding and forgave you for straying. What else can a wealthy, old man do when he's confined to a wheelchair?"

"There was nothing to forgive." Her chin lifted proudly as she met the obsidian glitter of his gaze.

"Wasn't there?" A brow arched. "We have two com-

completely and totally different opinions of fidelity."

"You won't even try to understand." Her shoulders sagged with the hopelessness of trying to explain.

"What happened between us is not something I'm liable to brag about, especially to John. Your secret is safe with me." His mouth thinned grimly. "As for you and Adam, I sincerely hope that John finds out what a two-timing tramp he has for a wife."

"Adam is engaged. He'll be married next month," Andrea declared angrily.

"That's a convenient red herring. It should throw John off the scent for several months. Maybe by that time you can find someone else to gratify your desires," Tell replied immediately without even a fraction's hesitation at her announcement.

Her chest constricted painfully. "How can you believe that?" she murmured.

"It's easy. I know you."

"You don't know me," Andrea protested numbly, making a slight negative movement of her head to one side. "You won't listen to me. You won't let me explain."

But Tell ignored her remarks, studying the glowing tip of his cigarette. "Mother and Nancy will be staying for two weeks as planned. I will find a convenient excuse to leave Sunday afternoon. You needn't worry." A slicing cynical glance swept over her. "I'll make sure it's believable so John won't realize that it's because I can't stand to be in the same house with his wife."

"Tell?" He was turning away to leave. Despite his

jeering wounding mockery and contempt, Andrea didn't want him to go.

"We have nothing more to discuss, Andrea," he said coldly.

Closing her eyes against the scalding tears, she breathed in deeply. "Would you tell John and the others that I'll be out in a few minutes?"

"My pleasure." His mouth curved with cynical politeness as he arrogantly inclined his head before walking away.

Tears were not permitted to fall. There wasn't enough time to hide the results for Andrea to give in to the pangs of self-pity and heartache. She used the delaying time to reassert a grip on her composure before walking to the veranda.

The conversation halted for a few minutes when she arrived, then began again as she took a seat on the wicker lawn sofa beside Nancy. Tell was sitting in the large wicker chair on the left, for the most part blocked from Andrea's vision by his sister. John and Rosemary dominated the conversation with reminiscences of past adventures. Andrea inserted a comment occasionally whenever she felt her silence had been too prolonged.

Tell didn't join in at all. If she hadn't been so sensitive to his presence, she might have forgotten he was there. But the wispy trail of cigarette smoke lazily twisting across the veranda would have reminded her.

In the latter part of the afternoon, John pivoted his wheelchair toward the house, announcing that he was going to look for an old photograph album with some early pictures of a party he and Rosemary had attended. Andrea immediately offered her assistance, but John waved her aside, choosing Rosemary to accompany him instead. Uneasily, Andrea leaned back against the sofa cushions, and no idle subject sprang to mind to fill the awkward gap left by John's departure.

"You have a beautiful home here," Nancy Collins said sincerely. "I've always loved this old house. Scott and I will probably never be able to afford anything like this ... not that I mind really," she added quickly with a contented and happy smile.

"John mentioned that you were engaged. Is Scott your fiancé?" Andrea seized on a means to keep the conversation going.

"Yes. His name is Scott Hanson." Proudly she held out her hand for Andrea to see her engagement ring, a small diamond solitaire with flanking emerald chips.

"How long have you known him?"

"About two years. Another boy took me to a fraternity dance, and Scott was there. The minute I saw him I knew that was it," Nancy said, beaming. "Of course, daddy didn't approve of him at first because Scott's background is so much different from ours. We didn't become officially engaged until last January when Scott graduated."

"When's the wedding?" Andrea inquired.

"Not until December," the young girl sighed, her large blue eyes revealing her regret at the long wait.

"That's a long courtship," Andrea offered sympathetically.

88

"Scott's working for an oil company right now. He's on sort of a probationary period. We're waiting until he's sure he has a job." A mischievous twinkle sparkled in her eyes. "And we want to make sure that daddy understands that Scott is not marrying me for the family fortune."

Tell pushed himself out of the chair, his sudden movement choking back the response that Andrea had started to make. With a lazy smile, he walked to stand in front of his sister. Unwillingly, Andrea tilted her head back to gaze up at him, drawn by the flash of his smile, but his gaze was cold when it sliced to her.

"It's commonly known as marrying for love, Mrs. Grant," he said with cutting softness. "I don't know if you're familiar with that motive."

She heard Nancy's quickly indrawn breath of shock. Wounded, Andrea tensed to keep the hurt from being shown too clearly in her expression.

"Are you, Mr. Stafford?" she countered.

"I'm a bitter believer in it," Tell answered dryly. "There's something I'm curious about. Can a man buy his wife's fiidelity with—" his hand reached out to touch the pearl choker, burning her neck, the flames reflected in her cheeks "—expensive jewelry?"

"Tell!" Nancy's horrified whisper begged him to stop.

"I wouldn't know, Mr. Stafford." Pride quivered in her voice. "John hasn't tried to buy mine."

"Maybe he knows he can't," he offered with jeering amusement, towering above her for an instant longer before he walked away, leaving the cobblestoned veranda for the landscaped lawn without another word.

At his departure, Andrea let her lashes flutter shut against the pain and pressed her lips tightly together.

"I'm sorry, Andrea," Nancy murmured.

She darted a glance at the knitted frown of concern on the girl's face, smiling faintly before she looked away. "It's all right, Nancy," she sighed. "I've become used to such comments."

It was a lie. Even the curiously raised brows of a stranger at her marriage to John had the ability to hurt. Tell's contempt and censure was nearly a mortal wound.

"It was unforgivable for him to speak to you that way!" Nancy's angry declaration was accompanied by a glowering look at her lean dark brother, now some distance away.

"My father once told me—" Andrea breathed in deeply "—that what you can't forgive, you must forget, and what you can't forget, you must forgive."

"Do you believe that?"

"I believe it." A smile curved bitterly inward. "I just don't know how to apply it." Brushing an imaginary strand of hair from her face, Andrea rose to her feet. "Would you excuse me, Nancy? I think I should see if Mrs. Davison needs any help in the kitchen."

"Of course. I understand."

Andrea didn't see Tell again until they all met in the living room before dinner. A glance at his granite face told her nothing. She couldn't guess whether she should be prepared to be ignored or subjected to his ridicule in front of others. The strain of not knowing what to anticipate was in the taut lines around her mouth while the agony of wanting his love and knowing he would never give it dulled her eyes.

"I see you've had the tennis court resurfaced, John," Tell commented.

"Yes, a couple of years ago," he acknowledged. "Andrea enjoys playing and the court had fallen into rather bad shape from lack of use."

Tell's mocking gaze slid complacently to her. "Where do you find your partners, Mrs. Grant? I somehow can't picture Mrs. Davison out there swinging a racket."

Her mouth tightened as she saw the quizzical look John gave him. "I have friends," she replied noncommittally.

"Adam and his fiancé come out occasionally," John explained, "but mostly it's her tennis instructor from Medford, Leslie Towers. She's quite good, Tell," he added with a touch of pride. "Maybe tomorrow if the weather holds, you and Nancy and Andrea can play a set."

"Maybe," Tell agreed lazily, his mouth curving into a cold smile. "It might be interesting to find out what kind of game she plays."

John missed the biting innuendo, but Andrea didn't. Judging by the dark blue anger that leaped into Nancy's eyes, she didn't, either.

"I hope she's good enough to beat you, Tell." It was small consolation to have his sister rushing to her defence.

"She's good, sis, but not that good," he said.

91

"Don't start bickering, you two," Rosemary Collins interrupted with a light laugh that revealed her ignorance of the undercurrents flowing between Andrea and Tell and intercepted by Nancy. "Why don't you get us a drink, Tell?"

"That's a good idea," John agreed. "I'll have a vodka martini."

"Is the bar still in the same place?" Tell inquired, allowing his mother to divert his attention from Andrea.

"It certainly is," John said, smiling.

Walking to the narrow side of the living room, Tell stopped in front of an ornately carved series of shelves, on which books and figurines were scattered. A series of pear blossoms had been carved on either side of the frame. He turned one of them and the shelves swung out to reveal cut-glass goblets of varying sizes and a supply of drink.

"I didn't know that was there!" Nancy exclaimed.

"I'm not surprised," her mother said. "The last time you were here, you weren't old enough to drink."

"I still never guessed it was there," she replied. "It's so artfully concealed."

"It used to be a cupboard," John explained. "My father had it converted into a bar complete with a refrigerator and a small mixing counter during the Prohibition days. He was so proud of it that I think everyone in the country knew it was there," he said with a very satisfied chuckle.

"This house, this entire area has seen a lot of things," Rosemary Collins commented idly, accepting the iced glass that Tell handed her. "A lot of gracious entertaining was done here. A lot of young men were sent to Medford in the early nineteen hundreds by their wealthy and strict parents from the East to mend their ways. Most of them stayed to build a new life. My grandparents had a summer home on the Rogue river. Every summer they'd leave San Francisco and spend it here. My mother attended St. Mary's Academy for a while."

"Yes, and in the winter there was a turnabout," John smiled, gazing into the martini Tell had given him. "My family would go to Carmel or Pebble Beach and we'd be entertained by your San Francisco friends. Of course, it wasn't all good times. I imagine there are some painful memories of the tent city that was erected in Medford for the survivors of the 1906 earthquake in San Francisco."

"But the stories that my mother told me of the theater and opera held here more than make up for that," Rosemary smiled, glancing at Nancy and Andrea. "Enrico Caruso performed here."

"That must have been something," Nancy mused.

"Here you are, sis." Tell held out a crystal glass.

She glanced up absently before accepting it. "Thanks."

Andrea held her breath as Tell turned toward her, meeting his hooded look reluctantly. His fingers were gripping the top of the glass, holding it out to her while making sure there would be no accidental contact when she took it from him. It hurt that he didn't want to feel her touch.

93

"I'm sorry, Tell," John spoke up quickly. "I forgot to mention that Andrea doesn't drink anything stronger than Coke."

She had been staring at the glass as she reached for it, finding it painful to meet his indifferent eyes. But at John's statement, her gaze was jerked to Tell's face. The glass was close enough for her to tell by sight and smell that it contained only Coke. He had remembered her aversion to alcohol and automatically served her an innocuous drink. His expression was grim as he returned her look.

"My mistake," he said curtly, withdrawing the glass from her hand. "I'll get you another."

"It looks like a Coke to me," Nancy observed innocently.

"With a splash of bourbon," Tell stated firmly. "You're not exactly the world's expert in alcohol, little sister."

"I should hope not," Rosemary said, laughing.

The incident was forgotten as John recounted a story of an early party. But it had been a slip that Andrea knew she wouldn't forget and she doubted that Tell would. She hadn't realized how easy it might be to make a mistake and betray the fact that she and Tell had met before. If John found out, she knew he would understand, but she didn't want to suffer the humiliation of having his family learn of it.

CHAPTER SIX

"I'LL PLAY the winner," Nancy declared.

Andrea tossed her light yellow jacket onto the fence. The nervous flutterings of her stomach were difficult to ignore as she shook her tennis racket free from its case. Tell was standing only a few feet away from her, bronze gold legs muscular and long beneath the drill white of his tennis shorts.

"How long has it been since you've played, Mrs. Grant?" he asked.

"Just this week," she answered tautly.

"Perhaps that will give you an advantage. I haven't played in over a month."

"Don't let him kid you, Andrea," Nancy warned quietly. "He's very good even when he's out of practice."

"I have no doubt of that." Andrea touched her hairband, making sure her hair was away from her eyes.

"John told me your instructor usually spends all afternoon out here. You must get in a lot of practice," Tell commented.

Stiffening, Andrea met his mocking gaze. "Sometimes we just sit and talk."

"About tennis?" There was a faint jeer in his tone.

"No, about a lot of other things."

"What business is it of yours anyway, Tell?" Nancy challenged.

"Just curious, my pet," he smiled coldly at his sister. "Considering the amount of time they spend together, I was just wondering how friendly Mrs. Grant was with her instructor, Mr. Towers."

"Leslie Towers and I are fairly good friends and quite close, Mr. Stafford," Andrea retorted. "Leslie is not only a friend but she's a female. So if you're through with your insults, lets play tennis. Shall I serve first or will you?"

Tell stared at her, hard, black eyes boring into her as if to seek some sign that she was lying. Andrea met them without flinching.

"What's the matter, Mr. Stafford? Are you disappointed to discover that I'm not having an affair with my tennis instructor?"

"Andrea." Nancy touched her arm in a placating gesture.

She sighed and bounced the ball to Tell. "You serve."

"Ladies first," he countered, flipping the ball back to her and walking to the near side of the court.

With his blazing return of the first serve, Andrea knew this would be no friendly tennis game. He intended to challenge her skill with every ball over the net. During the first set, she managed to stay close with the help of some lucky saves.

By the middle of the second set, as she chased his returns from one end of the court to the other, she knew he intended to run her into the ground. He was in command and on the offensive. Her defence was rapidly crumbling under the onslaught.

Lobbing a return to Tell, Andrea saw him set up for a blazing crosscourt smash. She ordered her tiring muscles to race to meet it. The ball was traveling at such a speed that there was only a slim chance that she could reach it. Stretching, she managed to get her racket on it, but her momentum sent her tumbling onto the court and the ball ricocheted off her racket and out of bounds.

Winded and beaten, she lay for a few precious seconds on the court. Her knee throbbed where she had grazed it in the fall. She pushed herself upright into a sitting position, breathing heavily from the exertion of the game. Overwhelming tiredness pounded through her, a physical and mental weariness that left her drained and vulnerable.

As she brushed the back of her hand over her forehead, her vision was momentarily blurred—whether by perspiration or weak tears, Andrea didn't know or care. Then Tell was towering above her, his dark gaze without even a glimmer of sympathy in their depths, glittering over her half-prone figure.

"Are you all right?" he asked with indifferent coldness.

Andrea swallowed the lump in her throat. "I bet you're sorry I didn't break my neck. But yes, I'm all right." She brushed at some imaginary dust on her pale yellow top.

"Give me your hand. I'll help you up," Tell ordered.

She stared at the tanned hand extended to her, wanting to feel his strong grip so desperately that it hurt. "No thank you," she said firmly.

97

"Give me your hand." It wasn't an offer. It was an order.

Glancing at his tightly clenched jaw, Andrea placed her trembling hand in his. Immediately, his hold tightened, and she felt the strength of his muscles easily pulling her to her feet. Whether or not it was accidental or deliberate on Andrea's part, the impetus carried her against his chest.

His hands quickly closed over her shoulders, keeping her there. Her head was tilted back to gaze into his face. Her heart raced like rolling thunder when she saw his dark eyes focus on her mouth.

Blind to everything but the rock wall of his chest, the pressure of his muscular thighs, the possessive grip of his hands and the glorious nearness of his masculine mouth, Andrea let a sparkle of hope and love shine in her eyes. His expression hardened. In the next instant he was roughly shoving her away, keeping only a steadying hand on her shoulder.

Why had she let him see? She blinked at the ground, humiliated that she had allowed herself to suffer his rejection again. She drew a shaky breath and shrugged free of his hand.

"Oh, Andrea, are you all right?" Nancy asked, coming to a breathless halt beside them.

"Of course she is," Tell answered. "It was only a little tumble."

"The game, set and match are yours, Mr. Stafford." Andrea's chin quivered in proud anger. "I declare you the winner."

"You've grazed your knee," Nancy observed.

"It's nothing," Andrea responded tautly as Tell accepted her declaration of forfeit without comment. "I'll put some antiseptic on it up at the house and it'll be fine."

"Would you like some help?" The large blue eyes expressed concern and sympathy.

"Don't waste your sympathy on her, Nancy," Tell cut in sharply. "Despite her fragile appearance, Mrs. Grant is quite hard underneath. She's more than capable of taking care of herself."

"How would you know?" Andrea retaliated bitterly. "You don't know anything about me."

His mouth thinned with hard cynicism. "I've met your kind before."

Scalding tears sprang to her eyes as Andrea turned abruptly away. Out of the corner of her eye, she saw Nancy's movement to follow her and the restraining hand Tell placed on her shoulder to stop her.

"Let her go, Nancy," he ordered in a low voice.

More words followed, but by then Andrea was too far away for them to be audible. She succeeded in slipping up the stairs to her room without being noticed. John and Rosemary were in the living room visiting, making up for lost years by bringing each other up to date on the happenings of their lives.

In the shower, Andrea didn't attempt to check the welling tears in her eyes, but let them mingle with the water spray. Later, wrapped in her short terry cloth robe, she sat curled in the center of her brass bed, her toweled head bowed, her hands resting listlessly on her crossed legs. Consciously, her mind was blank, but there was a whirl of torment around her.

There was a light rap on her door. "Who is it?" She rubbed any telltale traces of tears from her cheeks.

"It's me, Nancy," was the soft reply. "May I come in?"

"Yes, of course," Andrea replied, blinking several times, hoping there wasn't too much betraying redness in her eyes.

As the door opened, she pulled the towel from around her damp hair and began rubbing the strands in its folds. A faint smile was directed briefly at the girl who entered the room and closed the door behind her.

"I suppose your brother was the winner in your game, too," Andrea murmured dryly at the solemn look on Nancy's face.

"Of course. I ... I brought your jacket back. You left it on the fence," Nancy replied with a bright and forced nonchalance.

"Thank you. I'd forgotten all about it. Just toss it over the end of the bed. I'll put it away later."

There was a moment of hesitation. "That isn't why I came," Nancy sighed. "I just used your jacket as an excuse."

The drying motion of the towel stopped for a brief second before it started again, more vigorously than before. "What was it you wanted, Nancy?" Unwillingly, a wariness crept into Andrea's voice.

Sitting on the edge of the bed, the attractive young

100

woman stared at her hands, twisting them nervously in her lap. "I wanted to talk to you about Tell."

"Your brother?" Something cold froze in Andrea's chest, sending icy tendrils of fear through her system.

Nancy nodded mutely. "I know how insulting he's been toward you. I can't begin to apologize for the way he's behaved, but I want you to know that it's not your fault. He's not really picking on you."

"Isn't he?" Andrea responded grimly.

"What I mean is that he's not specifically singling you out. He seems to be—" Nancy paused, searching for the right word to explain what she meant "—contemptuous of all women, not just you. A few months ago he met this girl. I know I probably shouldn't be talking about it, but ... "

"It sounds very personal." Andrea could see where the conversation was leading. Somehow, she had to stop it. "You probably shouldn't tell me."

"No, I want you to know. Maybe if you do, his sarcasm won't hurt so much," Nancy explained, glancing anxiously at Andrea who slid to the side of the bed and walked to the dresser. "Each December, Tell arranges to take a long skiing weekend during the first part of the month before the Christmas rush starts at the stores. This last time he met a girl at Squaw Valley. Now, my brother is no saint. He's dated a lot of women and probably had affairs with several, but he's never really been seriously interested in any of them."

"Nancy, please." Andrea's fingers curled around a comb, the teeth biting into her palm. Thank goodness her back was to the bed and Nancy couldn't see the agony that she couldn't hide.

"Let me finish," Nancy insisted. "I want you to understand why he is the way he is. The morning of the day he came home, Tell called saying he was bringing this girl home for us to meet. He told mother to bring out the champagne so they could toast the girl he was going to marry. But when he came home, he was alone."

"Did ... did he tell you about her?" Unwillingly the question was asked. "Did he say what had happened?"

"He didn't say much about her on the phone except that she was the most beautiful woman in the world. He said we'd find out all about her when we met her. Of course—" Nancy breathed in deeply "—he didn't bring her home. Afterward, the only explanation he gave was that he had been lucky enough to discover what a cheap, scheming tramp she was."

Andrea winced. "I see," she murmured.

"He's become embittered and cynical because of her. When he lashes out at you, it's really that other girl that he's remembering," she concluded.

"Thank you, Nancy." Andrea had to speak softly to keep her voice from trembling with pain. "I do understand now."

"I know it isn't an adequate excuse for his behavior, but it is a reason," Nancy added hesitantly.

There was a moment of silence that Andrea was too choked to fill. Tell despised her so much.

"Well," Nancy sighed brightly, "I suppose I should go and shower and change before dinner. I think I have time.

What time are mother's friends supposed to arrive?"

"Er—" Andrea breathed in, biting her upper lip as she tried to reply calmly "—around six thirty. John planned to serve cocktails first and eat around seven thirty."

"I can hear it now." Nancy walked toward the door, a smile curving her cupid's bow lips. " 'My, Nancy, how you've grown! I hardly recognize you.' " With a grimace of resignation at her own mimicry, she opened the door into the hall.

Andrea wished that Nancy had not reminded her of the small dinner party that John was giving for Rosemary Collins. The only thing she wanted at this minute was escape. But escape was impossible. A plea of a headache or illness would perhaps be accepted by John or Nancy, even Rosemary. Tell would guess the truth and all of John's friends would draw their own conclusions.

She raised her eyes. When was all this going to end? Would it ever end?

Clenching her hands into fists, she vowed that she would make it through the evening. Neither Tell's contempt nor the hostility of John's friends would make her collapse. She owed it to John not to make a scene, not to embarrass him in front of others.

Standing beside his wheelchair that evening, a glass of ginger ale concealing the nervous tremors of her hands, Andrea glanced about the room, away from the older couple talking to John and excluding her from their conversation. It was always this way whenever John invited his friends.

Since she had married John, they had never attempted to hide the fact that they thought John had made a fool of himself. In front of him, they treated her with grating politeness; alone, they were more than rude: they cut her out completely.

That was true of all of his friends except two or three who had known Andrea's father and were more sympathetic to the circumstances surrounding their marriage. It made entertaining difficult. Andrea had tried not to let John see how much his friends upset her because she didn't want to deprive him of their company. After all, they were his friends and had been for years.

With a softly murmured excuse to John that she wanted to check on dinner, Andrea slipped into the dining room. She knew that under Mrs. Davison's expert touch there was no need to be concerned about the meal. But she was glad to escape the suffocating atmosphere of the living room if only for a few minutes.

Walking to the filmy lace curtains covering the windows where the gold drapes were drawn back, Andrea stared at her reflection in the night-darkened window. Wearily, she sighed, knowing that in a few minutes her disappearance would be noted and she would have to return.

"Aren't you enjoying the party?" Tell inquired mockingly.

Andrea pivoted swiftly. A minute ago she had seen him in the living room talking to Judge Simpson, retired now but still using the title. Quietly, he closed the double doors behind him.

"I ... I was checking on dinner," she said nervously, stepping toward the table and realigning the already straight silverware.

"Is that what you're doing in here?" he asked complacently. "I though perhaps you were bored. You hardly spoke to anyone in the other room."

"Correction. No one spoke to me." Andrea couldn't keep the bitter hurt from escaping. "You see," she explained, lifting her chin proudly, "John's friends have the same low opinion of me that you do."

"Including my mother?"

"No, not your mother and one or two others who knew my parents," she admitted. "But the others believe that I played on John's sympathy after my father died and tricked him into marrying me."

"Of course your father died penniless, didn't he? A series of bad investments just before his death wiped out the family fortune," Tell mocked. "Isn't that the way those sad tales of the beautiful heroine usually start?"

"There wasn't any money when my father died," Andrea admitted angrily. "I told you all about it before. When I was fifteen, the doctor told us that mother had cancer. There were operations, therapy, drugs, doctor and hospital expenses and a thousand other costly things. Despite everything, she died after nearly three years. Less than a year later, my father's heart simply stopped. But I never regretted one single dime he spent trying to save her."

"Which is why you married the first wealthy man who came along."

105

"John has more to offer than money." Her fingers nervously gripped the backrest of the mahogany dining chair.

"Such as?" His lip curled in a disbelieving sneer.

"He's strong and kind and understanding. He genuinely cares about me, about my happiness and well-being."

"Even to the extent of making you the main beneficiary in his will," Tell added. "That must have been a moment of real triumph for you."

Andrea let out her breath in one quick sigh and wearily bowed her head. "Why am I wasting my time? You don't want to listen. You don't want me to explain," she said dully.

"I'm curious about something, Andrea. What does John get out of all this? The privilege of having you as his beautiful paid companion?" he taunted, impassively meeting her flashing look of tears and temper. "There can be very little else, with you sleeping upstairs and John down."

She swung at his mocking face and missed as he dodged her open palm. One wrist was caught in a steel grip, then the other, cutting off the circulation to her hands. Andrea struggled in vain to be free.

"You're contemptible!" she hissed at last, no longer fighting his hold. "I don't care what you think of me! Not any more. Not if you can made such vile accusations against John. He's paralyzed, as you very well know. He didn't marry me to obtain some base satisfaction ... and that you think he did disgusts me!"

106

A muscle twitched along Tell's jaw, sternly clenched and unyielding. "When you love someone, Andrea—" his gaze narrowed blackly "—there is incredible joy in just knowing her head rests on the pillow next to yours. You couldn't possibly know the feeling I'm trying to describe. You're much too concerned about your own selfish, material desires to see the beauty and fulfilment in that."

Gasping back a sob of pain, Andrea knew it was something she wished for every night, but Tell wouldn't believe her.

"Excuse me, Andrea." Mrs. Davison's hesitant voice came from the doorway of the serving pantry connecting the kitchen and dining room.

Instantly, her wrists were released and Tell was stepping away. "Yes, Mrs. Davison," Andrea murmured in a choked tone.

"If they don't sit down to dinner pretty soon, that chowder isn't going to be fit to eat," the housekeeper replied.

"Thank you," Andrea smiled tightly. "I'll have the others come in right away."

"It can't be none too soon." And the pantry door closed behind the woman.

Andrea glanced hesitantly at the back of Tell's wide shoulders. "I don't think she was listening."

"And even if she was—" he turned his head slightly, letting the arrogant line of his profile be seen over his shoulder "—you'd be able to come up with some story to convince her nothing is wrong, wouldn't you? You

107

have the servants under your thumb as well as John, I suppose."

Andrea spun away. No matter what she said, Tell would not believe her. He was determined to think the worst of her and there seemed to be no way to stop it.

SLEEPING PILLS WERE a necessity that night. Even then Andrea lay awake for a long time before they took effect and brought that blessed unconsciousness.

The voices in the hall seemed part of a nightmare she was having in which a horde of accusing voices led by Tell were condemning her to a life of agony for not telling him the truth.

She struggled to raise the weighted lids of her eyes, confident that if she could open them, the voices would stop. They didn't. She tried to shut her ears to the sound. Finally the realization that she was hearing actual people penetrated her drugged stupor.

Clumsily, Andrea pulled on her robe and stumbled to the door. Shaking her head to clear her vision, she used the walls of the corridor for support to lead her to the sound. Near the top of the staircase, she saw Tell, his sister and Mrs. Davison. The two women were in house-coats. Tell was wearing a pair of dark slacks with an un-buttoned shirt covering his bare chest, as though he had put it on in a hurry.

"What's wrong?" she asked thickly, trying to push away from the wall and cover the short distance between them. Her legs wouldn't function properly and she had to sway back against the wall for support.

"For God's sake, what's the matter with her?" Tell muttered.

An instant later, Andrea felt his arms sliding around her, taking her weight against him while his hand closed over her chin and raised her face up for his frowning inspection.

"It's those sleeping pills she takes, I expect," Mrs. Davison answered in her usual low voice of disapproval.

"What does she need sleeping pills for?" Nancy asked curiously.

"To sleep. To sleep and not dream," Andrea responded softly, closing her eyes against Tell's nearness. His arm tightened around her for a second.

"Let's get her back to bed." The harshness of his voice made her wince, then she felt him bodily carrying her back to her room. But it was Mrs. Davison's face she saw as the covers were pulled over her arms and chest.

"Why is everybody up? What's happened?" Andrea asked, trying to sit up, only to have the light pressure of the housekeeper's hand push her back.

"It's nothing for you to worry about, dear," Mrs. Davison said gently. "Mrs. Collins had a slight asthma attack, but she's all right now. You go to sleep. I'll tell you all about it in the morning."

Andrea wanted to protest, but she felt herself slipping away. The bedside lamp was switched off and she remembered nothing else until the sun streamed into her window heralding the coming of morning.

As usual, her head throbbed dully as she dressed and made her way down the stairs. Her mind had begun to clear, enabling her to separate the dream of last night from the reality of what had actually transpired. In the downstairs hallway, she met Mrs. Davison on her way up with a tray.

Everyone is in the breakfast room," the housekeeper said, not slackening her step as she hurried by Andrea.

"Mrs. Collins?" she inquired anxiously.

"Much better," was the succinct response.

Reluctantly, Andrea turned toward the sunny breakfast area. She had the strange feeling that last night she had allowed Tell to see another chink in her armor and she was worried how he was going to use it to hurt her more. The first person she saw as she entered the room was John, smiling a greeting and letting her draw strength from his protective presence to meet the guarded look of Tell seated at the table beside him.

"Good morning." Her greeting was directed to all three and returned by Nancy and John. She avoided Tell's inspecting eyes to smile at Nancy. "How's your mother this morning?"

"She's fine," Nancy answered firmly and with a bright sparkle in her blue eyes that said she was telling the truth. "She gets these attacks every now and then, mostly when she becomes excited or overdoes things."

"I'm sorry I wasn't much help last night." Andrea self-consciously averted her attention to the coffee pot, only to find it in Tell's possession as he poured a cup and handed it to her.

"Tell said that you were a bit out of it," John commented.

110

"I, er—" she tossed her head back in a nervous gesture, smiling stiffly as she stared at the cup in her hand "—took a couple of sleeping pills before I went to bed last night. You know how they knock me out, John."

"Do you suffer from insomnia, Mrs. Grant?" Tell inquired in a bitingly soft voice.

"Occasionally," she shrugged.

"Quite often in the past few months," John corrected her dryly.

"Really?" A dark brow was arched across the table. "Are you suffering from a guilty conscience?" The question sounded innocently teasing, but Andrea knew better. Tell's arrows were swift and sure of their target.

"I had blamed it on spring fever," she countered.

"Thank heaven, I never have any trouble," Nancy sighed contentedly.

"That's because yours is the sleep of the innocent, kitten," Tell mocked, his remark ricocheting harmlessly off his sister to strike Andrea again.

"Is that why you work so late at nights, Tell?" Nancy teased in return. "You're lucky sometimes to have five hours' sleep out of twenty-four."

"What's your response to that, Mr. Stafford?" Andrea challenged.

"The plea of every man," he answered tautly, meeting her gaze and holding it. "Work, Mrs. Grant."

"Well," Nancy folded her napkin and placed it on the flowered tablecloth, "I'll leave you two to argue over the reasons for sleeping or not sleeping while I see how mother is doing."

"Give her my love," John said, wheeling his chair away from the table, "and tell her how very sorry I am that she wasn't able to join us this morning, but we'll be saving a place for her at noon, and I'm sure we're all hoping she'll be here."

"Knowing mother, she'll be down," Nancy said, laughing.

"I'll be up later," said Tell. When his sister had left, he glanced at the man in the wheelchair. "Would you like some more coffee, John?"

"No, no, I don't think so." The massive chest rose and fell as he took a deep breath. "If you want me, Andie, I'll be in my study."

When the whirr of the wheelchair faded, an awkward silence settled over the room. Tell poured himself another cup of coffee and rose from the table to walk to the window. A pulse hammered in Andrea's temple, not letting her forget he was still in the room. She spread homemade apple jelly over a slice of toast, trying to concentrate on it instead of the virile figure framed in the sunlight.

"This changes things," Tell said quietly, bending his dark head to stare at the cup in his hand. "You realize that, don't you, Andrea?"

"I'm afraid I don't follow you." Her knife was held poised above the toast, a frozen terror creeping through her limbs.

"I'm referring to mother's attack," he snapped. "It will be impossible for me to leave this afternoon as I'd planned."

112

"Of course," murmured Andrea, releasing the breath she had unconsciously been holding. Whatever she had been braced for, that wasn't it.

"Only for a couple of days, long enough to be sure she's all right. Believe me, I won't stay any longer than necessary," Tell muttered.

"There's no need to worry," she said stiffly. "I'm not likely to pretend that you're staying for any other reason than your mother."

Glancing over his shoulder, he glared at her coldly. Without another word, his long strides carried him from the room, leaving Andrea shaken and hurt, her head throbbing more painfully than before.

CHAPTER SEVEN

"ARE YOU SURE you don't want to come with us, mother?" Nancy asked again. "We're only driving over to Jacksonville, then into Medford to do some shopping."

"No, you and Andrea go." Rosemary Collins smiled. "I'm sure the two of you will have more fun without me. Besides, John wants me to read the rough draft of his novel so he can have my valued opinion." She glanced laughingly at John as if to say she was hardly a critic to be listened to. "This afternoon will be a good time for that."

"Well, if you're sure." Nancy shrugged and turned to Andrea. "If you're ready, I guess I am."

Touching John's shoulder, Andrea murmured, "We won't be late."

"Have a good time," he winked.

Adding a quick goodbye to Rosemary Collins, Andrea followed Nancy into the hall leading to the foyer. They had just reached the front door when a third pair of footsteps sounded in the hall.

Instinctively, Andrea turned, knowing it was Tell yet unable to prevent herself from looking. She had seen him so seldom in the past few days since his mother's attack. It did no good to remind herself that he was deliberately avoiding her. The bittersweet happiness of knowing he was in the same house and being able to catch an occasional glimpse of him was enough.

"Where are you off to, Nancy?" Tell said, frowning, a brow arching impatiently.

"Andrea and I are going to do some sightseeing and shopping. Why?" His sister's hand remained poised on the doorknob.

"Do I dare ask you to hold off leaving for an hour?" he asked with faint sarcasm.

"Why?" Nancy repeated tilting her head to one side.

"I have some correspondence that can't wait until I get back to San Francisco to be answered. I'd like to get it out this afternoon," answered Tell curtly. "I had hoped I could count on my sister's help since it's a family business."

"Dictation?" she asked with a grimace.

"And typing the letters," he acknowledged.

"You know how terrible I am, Tell," Nancy sighed, her hand falling away from the door. "Every time I help you, you always get so impatient. I can only take longhand and my typing is the two-finger variety."

His mouth thinned into a grim line as long fingers raked irritatedly though his black hair. "Never mind!"

"See, already you're snapping," his sister pointed out.

"Could I help?" The instant Andrea made the offer she wished that she could take it back as his smoldering dark gaze pinned her with sudden swiftness.

"Don't tell me you take shorthand and type?" he jeered.

"Have you forgotten that I told you I worked for

115

John?" Andrea demanded, trying to draw blood.

"That's not something I'm likely to forget, is it?" Tell responded with cold arrogance. "Of course, I couldn't be certain it was the truth either."

"It is the truth." Her reply was drawn tightly through the constricting muscles in her throat.

"I didn't know you worked for John, actual office work, I mean." Nancy turned a frowning, curious look to Andrea. "Where was I when you two were talking about that?"

In that stricken instant, Andrea realized that she and Tell had made another slip in their anger. Widened hazel eyes pleaded with him to rescue them, to satisfy his sister's curiosity before she became suspicious. His mouth tightened grimly, the clefts in his cheeks deepening with his inner displeasure.

"You were there, Nancy," he stated. "Obviously you were daydreaming about Scott again."

"That's possible," she acknowledged, a warm smile curving her mouth. "Are you going to accept Andrea's offer or are we going to struggle through those letters for the rest of the afternoon? With me helping, it will take that long."

His narrowed, resentful eyes slid over Andrea's tense face. "Since it's vital the letters are out today, I have very little choice. I'm practically forced to accept Mrs. Grant's offer. If you'll step into John's study, with luck your skill is such that we can be through with them quickly. I would hate to take up too much of your time and spoil your planned outing."

With the thinly veiled sarcasm of his last remark hanging in the air, Tell walked down the hall to the study. Feeling as if she were going to her own execution, Andrea hesitantly moved forward and Nancy followed.

"I hope it won't take too long for your sake," his sister offered, glancing toward the door Tell had left ajar, a wry grimace to her mouth. "He's in a vile mood today, as usual. Don't let him get you down, Andrea."

"I won't." But her smile was stiff. There was little ·chance that she would come out of the study unscathed.

Perhaps she was a masochist, Andrea thought idly, hesitating for a split second in front of the partially open door before pushing it open the rest of the way and entering the study. Tell was sitting behind the desk, shifting through a sheaf of notes lying on top.

Aware that he had deliberately not glanced up since she had entered, Andrea picked up her notepad and pencil from the typewriter stand that she used and walked to the chair in front of the desk. For several minutes, she sat there waiting for him to begin.

"I'm ready whenever you are," she said finally, the tension in the room oppressively suffocating her.

He leaned back in his chair, his brooding gaze centering on her with piercing thoughtfulness. Andrea wished she had not called attention to herself. He was deliberately attempting to unsettle her and he was succeeding.

Without any warning, Tell began the dictation, his low, clipped voice giving her the name, firm and address to which the letter was directed. Andrea had barely written that down when he began the contents of the letter.

She stretched her ability to the limit to try to keep up with his steady and swift dictation, but she slowly kept falling behind, relying on her memory to supply the sentences she had heard a moment ago while trying to concentrate on what he was saying. Finally, she had to acknowledge defeat.

"I'm sorry," she murmured, heat flashing into her cheeks as she refused to look up. "Would you repeat that last part? I'm afraid that I didn't get all of it."

"I thought you said you could take shorthand?" Tell challenged.

"Not at that speed," Andrea retorted. "If I could I'd probably be working as a secretary and not merely helping John from time to time." Even with her head downcast, she could feel his eyes boring into her, delving and examining.

"Why didn't you take some advanced training? Why didn't you get a job as a secretary? Why couldn't you have worked for John instead of marrying him?" The flurry of questions was hurled unwillingly, bitter frustration tightening his jaw and drawing his dark brows together.

"Why do you ask questions when you don't want to hear the answers?" Andrea cried, rising to her feet in agitation, knowing that no matter what answer she gave him, he wouldn't believe her.

Anger, blazing white-hot, pushed him from his chair. "How can you stand there righteously indignant, playing the martyr, pretending that you were the one who was betrayed? You were the one who lied to me! Who led me on! Who asked me to believe things that were untrue!"

"Tell, I was going to explain, I swear I was!" Andrea pleaded with him to believe her. "I even tried to do it the morning you came to my room, but you were too busy telling me what we were going to do that you wouldn't listen. I know if I had had the chance, I could have made you understand that things aren't as sordid and ugly as you think. Then John called, and you condemned me without hearing my side."

"And how does that explain the fact that you omitted to mention that there was anyone at home who had a prior claim? According to you, you didn't even have a boyfriend, let alone a husband," he taunted.

"If I'd told you I was married that first night we dined together, what would you have thought? We were strangers then. I wouldn't have told you the truth about the circumstances surrounding my marriage to John, not to a total stranger. But if you'd known I was married, would you have seen me again?" she demanded.

"No!" Tell snapped. "I'm disgustingly old-fashioned in that I believe the marriage vows between a man and a woman are sacred promises. I have little respect for those who don't keep them!"

Andrea recoiled from the venom in his voice as if she had been struck. "I haven't broken any promises I made to John," she murmured.

"Really?" he jeered. "How can that be when you promise to marry one man when you're still married to another? Is that something you promised John you would do?"

119

"I never promised to marry you!" Her hands trembled visibly as she cast the notepad and pen on the desk. "There isn't any point in continuing this conversation. You don't want to listen. You've become so twisted and cynical that all you want to do is hurt. You haven't even had enough courtesy to hear me out before you've judged me. I think I've been punished enough for my mistake without enduring any more of your insults!"

Spinning away from the desk, she hurried toward the door. Her eyes, already blurring with tears, turned the door into a dark mass and the brass knob into a shapeless, gleaming object. But Andrea wasn't to be granted a reprieve. As her fingers touched the cold knob, her shoulders were roughly seized and she was swung around with violent force.

"You don't know the meaning of the word 'punished'!" Tell snarled.

In the vice of his hands, Andrea was pulled toward his descending mouth. One quick gasping breath later, the punishing force of his kiss was bruising her lips, grinding them against her teeth until the taste of blood tainted her mouth. His arms then circled her, crushing her against his chest until she thought he intended to squeeze the air from her lungs.

Blackness swirled around her, but Andrea could not bring herself to be afraid. She loved him desperately and unendingly. Behind his brutal kiss, she knew that he loved her, too, although he despised and hated himself and her because of it. She was being smothered by his ravaging mouth and she didn't care.

When Tell drew his head away, relaxing his hold, she leaned weakly against his arms, too drained and defenceless to break free now that she had the chance. His eyes glittered over her like cold, black diamonds, cutting and emotionless. Then Tell released her completely and strode back to the desk.

"You may leave. I don't need your services any more," he said evenly. There was something in his calm dismissal that told Andrea that he was serious, that he meant it to mean forever.

Catching back a little sob, she fumbled for the doorknob, opened the door quickly and nearly tripped over the Irish setter whining anxiously on the other side. Andrea's fingers trailed lightly over his golden flame head in assurance that she was all right before she bolted for the stairs. In her room, she shed the tears she couldn't hold back.

More than a quarter of an hour later, her expression frozen by repeated applications of cold water to clear her red-rimmed eyes, Andrea walked down the stairs in search of Nancy. Her haunted eyes automatically sought the study door and veered away from the door tightly, and no doubt permanently, closed to her.

"Goodness! You're finished already!" Nancy exclaimed, quickly bounding from the chair beside her mother to hurry to Andrea's side. "You must have knocked Tell off his feet getting those letters done so soon."

It was the other way around, Andrea thought. She was the one who had been knocked off her feet, but she only smiled and asked Nancy if she was ready to leave. If Tell decided to let it be known that she had not helped him that was his business. Personally, she didn't want to explain how disastrously her offer had turned out.

"The last time I was in Jacksonville I was barely thirteen. I hardly remember anything but a lot of old buildings," Nancy chatted easily as Andrea started the car and turned it down the lane past the rows of pear trees. "Of course, the day before we had just taken a float trip over the rapids on the Rogue river. Anything would probably have seemed pale in comparison to that."

"The town has been classified as a National Historical Monument." Andrea was determined to keep the conversation from straying into a personal direction. This was to be a sightseeing trip and that was what they would discuss ... the sights they would see.

Ignoring the entrance ramp onto the fast, divided highway, she chose to take the leisurely and scenic back road from Gold Hill to Jacksonville. As they traveled the road with the pine-covered slopes of the mountains forever in the background, Andrea talked about the old stagecoach road and pointed out the thickets of blackberry bushes that would be heavy with large, succulent berries in late July.

When they arrived at the frontier town of Jacksonville, Oregon, there was a great deal more to attract Nancy's attention. Parking the car and taking a walking tour of the town, they turned off first down Oregon Street so Nancy could see the Brunner general store that the townspeople had used as a refuge during Indian raids, and the Oddfellows Hall across the street. The two feet of dirt between the roof and the ceiling of the latter structure had been installed to protect the building from fire in the event Indians attempted to burn it with a barrage of flaming arrows.

Other buildings possessed unique pasts as well. The Beekman Bank handled more than thirty-one million dollars' worth of gold, but never loaned any money in all its years of operation. The gold dust from the dance halls and gambling saloons had helped to fund the construction of churches in the town.

The better part of the afternoon was gone by the time they ended their tour with a walk through the old cemetery.

"Maybe Scott and I will come back in August to hear the Britt Outdoor Music Festival," said Nancy, voicing her thoughts aloud as they returned to their parked car.

"I go every year and enjoy it tremendously," Andrea responded, unlocking the door and sliding behind the wheel. She reached over to unlock Nancy's door.

"I'm much too content to go shopping. Let's go to Medford another day," she suggested.

"We still have plenty of time and it's not very far." Andrea glanced at her briefly as she started the car.

"Don't you feel relaxed and comfortable?" Nancy tipped her head inquiringly, a bright sparkle in her sapphire eyes.

"Very much so." Which was the truth. She had been able to carry off the day's excursion successfully without Nancy being the wiser about the scene with Tell.

"In that case—" the attractive girl settled into her seat, watching the scenery ahead as Andrea turned onto the road leading them home "—you can tell me all about the crazy argument you had with Tell just before we left."

"W-Wh-What?" The startled look she gave his sister nearly made her miss a curve in the road. Andrea had to turn the wheel sharply to keep from driving into the ditch. "What are you talking about?"

"Not even Superwoman could have got those letters out as quickly as you supposedly did," Nancy replied calmly. "And Tell was very anxious to get them out. Since you didn't have time to do them and considering the animosity he has expressed before, it had to have been an argument that got you free so soon." A faint smile dimpled one cheek. "Am I right?"

Andrea pressed her lips tightly together for a moment, then licked the lower one nervously. "Yes."

"What was it about this time?"

"The usual thing," Andrea shrugged.

"He's still on you about marrying John for his money," Nancy filled in.

"Something like that." There was a moment of silence the rural scenery couldn't make peaceful. Defensively, Andrea darted a glance at her fellow passenger. "Aren't you curious why I married a man who's not only old enough to be my father but is paralyzed as well?" she asked bitterly.

"To tell you the truth ...." Nancy paused then said emphatically, "Yes, I am curious. You are a very beauti-

124

ful woman, a fact you must be aware of. I would like to know why you married John, whom I dearly love myself. You're young and active. Would you mind telling me why?"

There was no sarcasm in Nancy's request, no prejudice against Andrea's reason. Curiosity was there and a desire to understand why Andrea had married John. In all her married years, no stranger had ever asked to understand. They had either jumped to conclusions or tolerated her presence as his wife, without beginning to think of what she might feel.

In spite of herself, a glimmer of tears welled in her eyes. If only Tell had reacted this way, how very differently things might have turned out.

Biting her quivering lower lip, Andrea smiled briefly at her companion in friendship. "Thank you, Nancy," she said tightly. "It means more to me than you'll ever know that you asked me to explain."

A gentleness entered the expressive blue eyes. "Will you tell me?" Nancy prompted gently.

Staring out the front windshield, Andrea began tentatively to relate the events that had led to her marriage: of her mother's long and futile fight against cancer, her father's death several months later, and of Dale's defection for another when she had needed most to know that she still had someone who cared. Nancy listened quietly, not interrupting but allowing Andrea to tell her story in her own way.

"Many people look at John and see an invalid, even some of his friends. When my father died, I saw the

125

indomitable strength that surrounded him. He was there, offering sympathy, comfort and compassion. He was understanding and kind. Most of all, he was patient: a trait Dale didn't possess, unfortunately," Andrea explained. "I had nowhere to go and no one to care. My mother did have some relatives in the Midwest, but they were strangers to me. There was only John and, in his own way, he needed me."

"Do you love him?" Nancy asked after waiting to be certain Andrea had finished.

"Not the way you love Scott," she acknowledged honestly, "but I do care for him. I would never hurt him."

"I should think not." The light airy note teased away the heavy seriousness that had dominated the last miles. "Now, I have something to tell you," Nancy announced with a smile.

Andrea's answer came naturally, warmed by a new bond of friendship established between them. "What's that?"

"I hadn't really looked forward to coming here. I dearly love John, as I told you, but I didn't know what I was going to do with myself for two weeks," Nancy explained. "Since I've come to know you, I'm really enjoying myself. I'll almost be sorry that I'll have to leave."

"I'm glad."

"Heavens, we're home already!" Nancy exclaimed as Andrea turned the car into the driveway. "It's about time, too." Laughter lurked in her soft voice. "We were on the verge of getting syrupy with our establishment of a mutual admiration society."

126

Andrea laughed. The two girls were still chuckling over an extension of the same thought by Nancy as they entered the house. Mrs. Davison was at the base of the stairs, with a huge bundle of freshly laundered towels in her arms.

"Now that's a nice sound." Her thin face nodded approvingly. "I've been waiting to hear that ever since Nancy arrived. Mrs. Collins and Mr. Grant are in the living room. Dinner won't be for another hour and a half."

"My brother is still sulking in the study, is he?" Nancy flashed an amused glance at Andrea who looked hesitantly at the closed door, unable to smile at the memory of their argument.

"Mr. Tell? He's gone," the housekeeper replied in a tone that implied she thought they had known.

"Gone?" His sister tilted her head inquiringly to the side. "What do you mean 'gone'? Gone where?"

"Well, back to San Francisco, of course."

Andrea's small bubble of happiness was instantly deflated by the housekeeper's words. Tell had left and he wouldn't be back.

"Did he say why?" Nancy frowned.

"Not to me, miss." The housekeeper started up the stairs.

"That's strange," Nancy mused aloud, turning absently toward the living room, conscious that Andrea followed but not noticing the pallor that had taken possession of her face. "Tell hasn't even hinted that he might have had to go back without us." She glanced briefly at

127

Andrea. "Did he mention anything about it to you this afternoon?"

His departure hadn't been discussed this afternoon, although she had known he intended to leave as soon as he was convinced his mother was better. That part she ignored.

"He didn't mention it at all," she answered, invisibly crossing her fingers at the near white lie.

"Maybe mother knows what's going on," Nancy murmured as they walked through the living-room.

"There you two are! We didn't expect you back for another hour." Rosemary Collins was sitting on the couch, looking youthful and elegant in a dress of pale yellow. "Did you have a good time?"

"A very good time," Nancy said emphatically.

The Irish setter, keeping his vigil beside John's wheelchair, slapped his tail against the floor in greeting. "I don't see any packages," John observed. "I thought you two girls were going to buy out the town."

"We spent all of our time in Jacksonville," Andrea explained, hoping the warm gray eyes examining her face didn't comment on its paleness.

"Yes, we're saving our shopping expedition for another afternoon," Nancy added, sitting on the cushion next to her mother.

Andrea could see the beginnings of the question about Tell forming on his half-sister's lips. She wasn't anxious to be an actual part of the conversation. Not when she wasn't certain she could keep her reactions to the answers from being seen.

"Would any of you like a cocktail?" she asked quickly before Nancy had a chance to speak.

"A sherry for me," Nancy requested, followed by John's and Rosemary's preferences.

Andrea was at the concealed bar, separated from the others as Nancy began asking about Tell.

"Andrea and I saw Mrs. Davison in the hall," she said. "She told us Tell left for San Francisco. It was a bit sudden, wasn't it?"

"Yes, he left quite abruptly," her mother sighed. "He said some problems had come up that couldn't be handled from here."

"Is he coming back?" Nancy asked.

"He said if he couldn't get back, he'd make arrangements for us."

"Which means he won't be coming back," she concluded grimly.

"That was the impression I had, too," Rosemary agreed.

Andrea closed her eyes briefly against the stabbing words, then opened them to measure out the vodka for John's martini. Indirectly, she had driven him away by the very fact that she was here, she thought to herself sadly.

"It's funny," Nancy said with a frown. "When daddy called the other night, he said everything was going smoothly. I even teased him about saying that so you and Tell wouldn't worry, but he insisted that it was amazingly true. I wonder what difficulty arose that daddy couldn't handle alone?"

129

"I'm curious about that, too." Rosemary Collins studied the armrest of the sofa, displaying an intense interest in the pattern of the colored threads. "I can't shake the feeling that it has something to do with that girl. I hope my mother's intuition is playing tricks on me. As badly as he was hurt the last time, I hate the thought of Tell seeing her again, no matter what the reason."

The glass nearly slipped from Andrea's hand. Her stomach turned at the thought of Nancy's and Rosemary's reaction should they ever learn she was the girl to whom they were referring with such bitter dislike.

"Oh, mother, you don't suppose she had the nerve to contact him again, do you?" Nancy was plainly astounded and outraged by the thought.

"I certainly hope not!" was the emphatic response.

"Now, now," John mildly reproved their harshness. "I don't think anyone could make a fool of Tell twice."

"But he was so very much in love with her," Rosemary sighed.

"People recover from broken hearts," John replied in his wisest voice. "You simply have to be patient."

"Did you recover, John?" Rosemary asked with soft sadness.

"Yes," he breathed in deeply. "I recovered, a bit scarred but as good as new otherwise." He patted the arm of his chair as if wishing the conversation was on another subject. Then he glanced over his shoulder at Andrea. "Do you have the drinks ready yet? She isn't the world's most adept bartender, but I keep her around anyway."

130

"Coming right up," she replied with brittle brightness.

As Andrea carried the small tray with the drinks to the others, she remembered that time several years earlier when John had confided that he had once lost the woman he loved. He had not explained the circumstances, but Andrea had had the impression that the woman had chosen another.

It had been an admission he had made shortly after Dale had broken their engagement. Until this minute, she had thought he had said it to make her feel better and more able to face the future. For some reason, she hadn't thought it was actually true. Now she realized from Rosemary's comment that he really understood her misery.

Knowing that made her feel much closer to him. She drew new strength from his presence, holding her head up higher when it wanted to bow in defeat at the knowledge that she would never see Tell again.

CHAPTER EIGHT

AFTER DINNER THAT EVENING, there was a telephone call for Nancy from her fiancé. Nearly a half an hour later, she came gliding out of the study, where she had taken the call in private, seeming to walk on air. Her large blue eyes shimmered with a dewy-eyed rapture that tugged poignantly at Andrea's heart.

"Are you here or floating somewhere above us?" she asked lightly, swallowing back the bitter taste of envy.

"Somewhere above," Nancy beamed. Then she hugged her arms tightly around herself. "Oh, Andie, I miss him so much! It's just awful being away from him, even for two weeks," she moaned.

"I'll bet the feeling is mutual." There was a wistfulness in her smile.

"He doesn't talk about his feeling very much. He's kind of shy about putting it into words, but I like it that way," Nancy said, smiling, tears of happiness glittering in her love-radiant eyes. "Because when he says he loves me, I know how very much he means it."

"I'll take a guess and say that Scott uttered those three precious words not too long ago. Am I right?" she added, laughing hollowly.

The haunting memory of Tell's husky voice, vibrating with deep emotion, and whispering those same precious words, echoed clearly in her mind. Pain throbbed dully in her breast to know just one more minute of his love.

"Oh, you know he did!" Nancy's smile spread across her face. From the living room where John and Rosemary were, the sound of a strident female voice caught Nancy's attention. "Who's in there with mother?"

"A Mrs. Van Ryden. She was a friend of your mother's when they were younger. She's visiting locally and heard that Rosemary was staying here, so she dropped over to see her," Andrea explained.

"Do you suppose it would seem terribly rude if we sneaked to my room rather than joined them?" There was a mischievous glint in Nancy's expression.

"I don't think we would be missed." With a toss of her dark gold hair, Andrea turned toward the staircase.

Carefree hours were spent in Nancy's room, indulging in girl talk. Even while she enjoyed it, Andrea discovered a bittersweet pain in hearing Nancy's plans for her wedding, but she entered into the talk with spirit, only guarding her tongue when Tell was mentioned.

As much as she liked and trusted Nancy, she could not trust her with the truth of her previous relationship with Tell. She and Tell were half-brother and sister. The blood ties would naturally be strong.

IT WAS AFTER ELEVEN when Andrea slipped from Nancy's room. Rosemary had come up nearly an hour before that. The entire house was quiet. Tiptoeing down the stairs, she whistled softly for Shawn, the setter, to take him for his nightly walk. He padded quietly to her side as if sensing the need for silence in the sleeping house.

133

Out the veranda doors and into the garden, Andrea walked. The dog trotted at her side for several yards before ambling off to investigate the yard. The air was faintly brisk and cool, the breeze coming down from the mountains bringing the fragrant scent of pines to mingle with the blossoms in the orchard. The sky glittered with stars, a crescent moon suspended in one corner.

There was a lonely peace in the cool night. A promise of romance lay in the shadows, but Andrea was alone. She sighed, telling herself that she might as well get used to the feeling. Nights like this were meant for couples and she was out here walking the dog.

A wry smile pulled up the corners of her mouth as she whistled for Shawn. A few seconds later the setter was trotting out of the dark, moonlight shimmering over his bright coat. He pushed his nose against her hand in greeting, then turned toward the house. As always, he was anxious to get back to John.

In the house, Andrea took the corridor leading to the master bedroom, but the setter didn't follow. She glanced back, surprised. He was looking at her anxiously, then toward the hallway. Andrea frowned, then realized that John had evidently not gone to bed and was somewhere in the house.

"Okay, Shawn," she smiled, retracing her steps. "Where is he?"

With a whine of gladness, the setter whirled quickly around, making straight for the closed study door. Only a flicker of light gleamed beneath it. Andrea tapped once, waiting for John's response before entering.

There were no lights on in the room, but the setter made his way to the wheelchair with unerring accuracy. A fire had been lit in the fireplace some time ago. Red coals were all that remained with an occasional, tired flame springing to life only to fade into the embers.

The faint red glow strangely made the wings of gray in John's hair seem more silvery and white. He was staring into the expiring fire, his strong face heavy with concentration. Andrea walked quietly toward him and stood behind him, placing her hands on his shoulders.

"It's getting late, John," she prodded gently.

He patted one of her hands, then clasped it and drew her around in front of him. "I'll be turning in shortly," he said and smiled faintly as she settled onto the floor beside him.

"What's wrong?" Andrea asked quietly, her hand still held in his.

"Nothing," he sighed.

"Something is troubling you—I can tell. Now what is it?" Her voice was soft, wanting to reach out to him as he had to her so many times in the past.

"Oh—" he drew his gaze away from the fire with an effort "—I'm afraid I put my foot in it this time."

Her brows drew together curiously. "What do you mean?"

His mouth tightened ruefully. "I finally got up enough nerve this morning to comment to Rosemary on Tell's less than agreeable behavior. She told me about his misfortune with love this year."

Just 'this year'? Andrea wondered. Had Rosemary

given him no specific dates and places that might enable John to put two and two together and come up with Andrea and Tell? She held her breath, waiting to see if he was going to ask the crushing question.

"She asked me to talk to him. Everyone else had tried, but no one had got through his armor of bitterness. So I talked to him this afternoon, shortly before he left."

"And?" The darkness of the study hid her tense expression.

"And I'm the one who prompted his sudden departure," John concluded with a heavy sigh. "I shouldn't have interfered."

"Don't say that," Andrea protested.

"Why shouldn't I say it? Tell did," he encountered with rueful lightness.

"What did he say?" She bent her head, apprehension lurking like the darkness of night waiting to rush in when the last glow from the fire died.

"I barely got out what I wanted to talk to him about when he cuttingly informed me that he wasn't about to be lectured by me. I tried to explain, as I did with you, that losing at love should make a person stronger, not harder. That's when he told me that he was leaving and that he doubted he would be back and would I kindly refrain from discussing his personal life in future."

Andrea let out her breath slowly. The last request had been issued as a means to protect both of them from discovery. It was cold comfort.

"You tried, John," Andrea murmured, remembering

with an ache the time she had tried to explain to Tell and was turned away. "It isn't your fault he wouldn't listen."

"No, I suppose not. But a person always wonders that if he handled it differently, the end result might have been changed." Regret entered his voice.

"It's late." She struggled to her feet. "It's time we both were in bed. Would you like some help?"

"No, you go on. I'll stir out the fire, then push myself off to bed." He waved her offer aside before reaching for the poker and wheeling his chair to the firescreen.

"Good night, John."

"Good night, Andie. Thanks for listening. I only wish Tell had."

"Sometimes people feel that they have to find their own way without any help," she suggested, knowing that she had been unable to turn to John this time as she had done in the past.

"You sound very wise," he said as he smiled.

"I learned from you how to stand and walk with my head up," Andrea reminded him. It had been one of the most important lessons she had learned.

"I'm glad. I'd hate to think that I had made a mess of your life."

"You couldn't do that." Wishing him another good night, Andrea opened the study door and walked into the hallway.

The sleeping pills were slow to work their magic that night. Tell was gone. No matter how she tried to push that fact from her mind, it kept slipping back. The first time they had parted, she had cried with heartbreak. This second time, she knew a pain beyond tears. If there had ever been any hope that someday they might meet again and rekindle the love they had shared, it had died with this second meeting.

To live without a dream was a frightening prospect. Andrea wished she could cry for herself and her future. She blinked her dry eyes, but they remained parched.

IT WAS THE HEAVENS that cried for her—slow, steady tears of rain gloomily dampening the earth. Melancholy gray clouds blocked out the sun for two straight days. There was a mourning hush to the world outside. The breeze stopped playing in the trees and the mating calls of the birds were silenced. There was only the rhythmic pitter-patter of the tears falling from the clouds.

Nancy was standing at the window, gazing out at the unchanging scene of steadily drizzling rain. Thrusting her hands in the pockets of her slacks, she turned away.

"I thought the San Francisco fog was depressing sometimes, but it has nothing on this." Her hand made an impatient gesture toward the window.

"Come over here," her mother suggested. "It's much cheerier by the fire."

Obligingly, Nancy walked over to stand in front of the friendly, crackling flames. She stared into them for long minutes, then sighed again.

"I wish Scott would call," she said.

"Nancy, you're becoming as moody as the weather!" Rosemary smiled and shook her head, barely glancing up from the needlepoint in her lap.

138

"After two days, I'm not surprised that it's rubbed off on to me," she retorted.

"Why don't you find yourself a book in John's study and read? It's a perfect day for it. Mrs. Davison is making some cocoa. It'll be here in a few minutes," Rosemary Collins replied, then glanced at Andrea. "What are you reading, Andrea?"

She had been aware of the conversation between mother and daughter, but she wasn't paying attention. The sound of her name stopped her wandering mind from thinking about Tell and what he might be doing, and forced it to concentrate on the people around her.

"I'm sorry," Andrea murmured self-consciously. "What did you say?"

"That must be a good book." A brow was arched lightly in a teasing look as Rosemary repeated her question. "What are you reading?"

The book had been lying open in her lap at the same page for so long that Andrea couldn't remember which book she had taken from the shelf. Nervously she flipped the pages to the front of the book.

"It's a collection of short stories by Hemingway," she answered.

"I don't think she's been reading at all," Nancy said laughingly as Andrea shifted her position on the seat cushions of the bay window. "I think she's been staring out the window, daydreaming."

"Mostly," Andrea admitted with a slightly red-faced smile.

"I'm not in the mood to read, either," Nancy stated

139

emphatically. "And after playing solitaire nearly all of yesterday afternoon and discovering on the last game that there were only fifty-one cards in the deck, I'm not in the mood to play cards, either. Do you know how impossible it is to win with the ten of spades missing?" she asked with a rueful laugh.

Closing the book in her lap, Andrea sat it on the cushion beside her, swinging her stockinged feet to the floor. Now that she had been drawn into the conversation, it was impossible to ignore her duties as hostess despite the private sorrows of her heart. The rest of her life was ahead of her. There would be more than enough time to remember those precious days with Tell, and to learn how to endure the aching loneliness of trying to live without him.

Mrs. Davison walked into the living room with a tray. Marshmallows bobbed in the rich, steaming mugs of cocoa.

"Would you be wanting any cookies or cake?" she asked as she set the tray on the rectangular marble table in front of the sofa.

"All I've done since it started raining is eat," Nancy sighed. "Please don't bring any food or I'll have to spend the next month dieting to lose the weight I've gained." A mischievous twinkle entered her eyes. "There are only three times that I overeat, as mother will tell you. One is when it's raining. Two is when I have nothing to do and the last is when I'm missing Scott. So you see, I'm in real trouble."

"Please, Mrs. Davison, no snacks," her mother

agreed. "It's bad enough hearing her complain that she has nothing to wear without hearing her moan that her clothes don't fit!"

"Very well, miss," the housekeeper smiled faintly. "The weatherman said there'd be a chance of showers tomorrow, though, so there'll be no immediate hope for two of her problems."

Nancy gave an expressive groan of dismay.

"What about a game of backgammon?" Andrea suggested. "Do you play?"

"Sounds great!" the brunette endorsed the suggestion, pushing the silky fine hair from her face.

"I'll go and get the board." Andrea set her mug of cocoa on a coaster and went in search of the backgammon set.

They were in the thick of the first game, sitting on the floor in front of the fireplace with the board balanced on their laps, when Andrea spied Shawn out of the corner of her eye as he investigated her mug of cocoa. Quickly she pushed it out of reach of the setter's questing nose.

"Be sure your cup is out of reach," she warned Nancy. "He's crazy about marshmallows, especially if they're half-melted in hot chocolate."

"His one major fault," said John, entering the room after the setter. "He knows he's not supposed to, but he'll knock over a cup of cocoa just to get the marshmallows. Won't you, feller?" he asked the dog, which was gazing adoringly back at him, wagging its tail slightly as if in apology for the weakness in its character.

"Everybody has their faults, even dogs," Nancy observed. "Mine is my inability to beat anyone at backgammon."

John wheeled his chair closer. "Is that what you're playing?"

"Yes, and naturally Andrea is winning." The dice dropped from the girl's hand and rattled across the board.

"I'm not much good at games," he commented after watching them play for a few more minutes. "Andrea has been trying to teach me backgammon ever since she learned it last winter."

"You certainly had a good teacher," Nancy sighed, studying the board with a frown. "Who was it? I'd like to sign up for a few lessons about now."

Swallowing nervously, Andrea smiled and pretended that the question had been asked in jest and didn't require an answer. She couldn't very well tell Nancy that her own half-brother had taught her the game.

"It was somebody you met at Squaw Valley who taught you, wasn't it, Andie?" John asked curiously.

"At Squaw Valley?" Rosemary glanced up from her needlework with a frown. "John, you surely didn't make the trip to Squaw Valley last winter, did you? They have six to eight feet of snow there and more. How could you possibly get around?"

"I didn't go. Andrea went on a skiing holiday," he explained.

"Alone? Without you, John?" The older woman's frown deepened.

The thinly veiled disapproval in her voice brought a

hint of embarrassed pink to Andrea's cheeks. She kept her gaze downcast, but she felt Nancy's eyes inspecting her face.

"Heavens, mother," Nancy defended, "there's nothing wrong with wives going somewhere without their husbands. Look at you. Right now you're here without daddy."

"Well, yes ...." But the unfinished comment indicated that Rosemary thought the circumstances were entirely different.

"Our whole family used to go quite often." Nancy began to talk lightly to ease the faint tension that had sprung into the air. "Were you there during the Christmas holidays? We spent one Christmas there. It was so crowded that skiers were nearly bumping into each other on the slopes."

"No, I don't like to be away from home on Christmas," Andrea hedged, not admitting when she was there.

"I suggested," John spoke up, "That she go over the New Year's weekend so she could celebrate with some young people instead of staying home with me, but she insisted on taking her trip on the first of December."

"The first of December?" Nancy repeated, astonishment parting her lips. "Andrea, that's when Tell was there!"

"Was where?" Andrea, asked blankly.

"At Tahoe. At Squaw Valley, to be more precise. He took his holiday there the same time as you. Isn't that a coincidence?"

Yes, it is." Andrea passed Nancy the dice, hoping to distract her attention back to the game.

But Nancy clutched the dice in her hand, her expressive face reflecting the thought that had flashed across her mind, expectant and anxiously excited. "Did you see him?" she whispered.

For a minute Andrea wanted to pretend that she didn't know who Nancy meant, but she didn't think she would be believed.

"No, I didn't." She shook her head. "It's your turn."

Nancy rolled the dice around in her hands, a thoughtfulness invading her eyes. "Isn't it strange that you didn't see Tell? You didn't see him, did you?"

"Your brother is hardly someone I would forget had I ever met him before he came here," Andrea lied. Her heart seemed to stop and start a hundred times, especially when the light in Nancy's eyes became vaguely suspicious.

"Where were you staying?"

"I rented an apartment for a week." That was a half-truth anyway, but she needed something more to convince Nancy. "Considering all the people who were there at the time, it's really not surprising that I didn't meet him. Besides, I kept to myself—I didn't really go out and socialize."

"No, I suppose not." The agreement was made with reluctance. "Tell really enjoys playing backgammon. Like everything else, he's very good at it," Nancy commented.

The very fact that she didn't glance at Andrea seemed

to say that she hadn't completely given up the notion that Andrea and Tell might have met. Outwardly, Andrea appeared composed and interested only in the game they were playing. Inside, she was quaking like an aspen leaf in a storm.

"It's getting to be a very popular game," was Andrea's smiling response. "And it's still your turn."

"It's no wonder you hardly ever win, Nan," her mother teased. "You start talking and your mind gets off on another track. You have to learn to concentrate on what you're doing."

There was a brief moment when Andrea thought Nancy wasn't going to let the subject drop and a cold chill of dread raced down her spine. But it wasn't brought up again. Still, there was a wary curiosity in Nancy's expression each time she glanced at Andrea, as if she guessed that Andrea had not told her the truth. Andrea realized there was a stubborn streak in Nancy just as there was in Tell. She doubted very much if she had heard the last of Nancy's questions.

With that fear haunting her, Andrea stayed close to John and Rosemary for the rest of the afternoon, not allowing Nancy any opportunity to maneuver her into a private talk in case Andrea made some slip that might give her away. It was hard to do because she liked Nancy very much. She just couldn't take the chance of arousing the girl's suspicions again, since Nancy was so clever.

At half past four, Adam Fitzgerald called at the house to see John on business. Andrea answered the doorbell, smiling a relieved welcome at the sight of his familiar face. He handed her a small paper sack as he walked in the door.

"What's this?" Andrea frowned curiously.

"I called in at the drugstore and Sam, the pharmacist, sent it with me. He said you'd asked to have it delivered," Adam replied.

In the confusion of the near discovery by Nancy, Andrea had forgotten that she had telephoned the pharmacy that morning to have her prescription for the sleeping tablets refilled. Pulling her mouth wryly at her forgetfulness, she took the package and set it on the foyer table for the time being.

"Of course it is for me," she admitted. "I guess I didn't expect you to be bringing it."

Adam tilted his head to the side. "You look pale. Aren't you feeling well?"

"I'm fine," Andrea said hurriedly. "I just haven't been getting much sleep lately, that's all."

"Are you still having that problem?" he said, frowning in concern.

She forced the tense muscles in her face into a smile. "It's more of an inconvenience than a problem," she shrugged.

"Does John know you take them?"

Of course he does. I don't keep it a secret."

A sandy brow arched slightly at her defensive tone, but Adam let the subject drop as Andrea turned toward the living room. "Is John in there?" he asked.

"Yes."

"Would you have him meet me in the study?" he

146

requested turning toward the corridor that led to the paneled room.

"Adam," Andrea spoke hesitantly, "if you don't have anything planned would you join us for dinner this evening?" The longer she could keep a barrier between herself and Nancy, the better her chances would be that Nancy might forget her suspicions and Andrea would be safe again.

"As a matter of fact, I'm at a loose end this evening." His cheeks dimpled in a regretful smile. "Carolyn is babysitting with her sister's children tonight."

"Good." Andrea breathed a silent sigh of relief. "I'll tell John you're in the study and have Mrs. Davison put an extra potato in the pot. After almost three days of being imprisoned in the house by the rain, a fresh face is what we all need at the dinner table tonight."

"There's supposed to be more of the same tomorrow," he grinned.

"Don't remind me," she laughingly said over her shoulder as she started into the living room.

With the message given to John, Andrea excused herself immediately to go to the kitchen to inform Mrs. Davison of the extra person for dinner.

"So Adam's invited himself to dinner, has he?" was the housekeeper's gruff response to Andrea's announcement. "I don't think that boy cares much for his own cooking. I'll be glad when he gets married and I won't have to keep juggling the portions."

"I invited him," Andrea explained. "I thought it would be a nice break from the routine. Can I help?"

"The way you've been mooning about the house since Mr. Tell left, you wouldn't be of much help to me in the kitchen," Mrs. Davison retorted. "You'd be in the middle of something and forget what you were doing."

The last of the housekeeper's words didn't penetrate. Andrea was frozen by the woman's initial statement. The thin-faced woman glanced at her briefly, her shrewd eyes taking in Andrea's pale face and shocked expression.

"Housekeepers inadvertently see and hear things they're probably not supposed to, Andrea," Mrs. Davison said quietly, maintaining the rhythmic stroke of the vegetable brush over a carrot.

"The night of the dinner party . . . you heard us talking in the dining room?" Andrea swallowed tightly, hoping the woman would deny it.

"I heard enough to guess that you hadn't met him for the first time in this house," she answered.

"I see." Andrea stared at her hands, twisting them nervously in front of her. "And what do you propose to do about it?"

"Me?" The housekeeper shrugged. "I don't plan to do anything about it, or the expensive ring upstairs in your drawer. I'm just wondering what *you're* going to do about it."

"You ... You know about the ring too?" Andrea asked in a stricken voice.

"I found it by accident." The thin face was softened by a sympathetic smile. "Haven't you told Mr. Grant?"

"You must have realized that it wouldn't make any difference, Mrs. Davison." With a supreme effort to gain control, Andrea tossed her hair, lifting her chin proudly. "And I've already been enough of a burden to John without going to him with more of my sorrows."

The housekeeper sighed. "It's for you to decide. I won't be saying a word. I probably shouldn't have opened my mouth to begin with, but I watched you silently grieving for your parents and that no-good boy you were engaged to. The haunted look was just leaving your eyes when you went on that holiday last winter. I've grown fond of you, child." Her eyes anxiously searched Andrea's taut face. "It hurts me to see the pain back."

Andrea pressed her trembling lips together, touched by the concern and affection expressed by the usually restrained woman. "Thank you, Mrs. Davison, but everything will work out."

"There, I've gone and upset you." The woman smiled in genuine regret. "Why don't you go upstairs and take a long, hot bath? I'll make sure no one disturbs you."

"I think I will." Andrea knew she was in no condition to return to the living room. Her precarious composure would not stand up under Nancy's scrutiny or any probing examination of her holiday in Tahoe.

CHAPTER NINE

ADAM'S PRESENCE at the dinner table that evening was a godsend for Andrea. His easy, outgoing personality kept the conversation on impersonal topics. It had taken little argument to persuade him to stay for part of the evening. When he finally left, a peaceful quiet settled over the house and Andrea knew she didn't need to be afraid that Nancy might bring up the subject of her brother again, at least not that night.

By ten o'clock, everyone had retired to their respective bedrooms. As Andrea creamed the make-up from her face, the carefree mask she had worn that evening was slowly removed at the same time. Her large, hazel green eyes reflected the pain from within. Even the dark gold of her hair seemed less bright. Staring down at the birthstone ring, which was her wedding band, she touched the two stones that had been remounted the previous winter. Slowly, she removed the ring from her finger and laid it on the dressing table.

Walking to the dresser, she reached into the corner of one of the drawers and took out the small jeweler's box hiding in the back. Strangely, the silver gold band was warm as she slipped it on her finger. The rainbow colors of the diamond solitaire sparkled mockingly into her face.

"I'll only wear it again this once," Andrea whispered

in a promise to herself. "Only for a little while." Folding her hands together, she carried the ring to her lips, closing the gold tips of her lashes against the acid dryness of her eyes. "I love you so, Tell," she murmured achingly.

Walking to the curved window on the mock tower side of her room, she stared into the black drizzle of the night. Her mind's eye saw a mountain of white snow and Tell leaning on his ski poles, his dark eyes crinkling at the corners to match the warm smile on the masculine mouth, raven black hair glistening with the brilliant blue hues of the Sierra sky.

For long moments, she allowed the image to dominate her mind before turning away from the window with a dejected sigh. The turned down covers on the brass bed weren't at all inviting to Andrea, but neither was the prospect of remaining awake with her thoughts.

With another sigh, she walked into the adjoining bathroom and opened the medicine cabinet. Then she remembered that her new supply of sleeping pills was still on the table in the foyer. Frowning that she hadn't remembered them before, she reached for the short terry robe on the door hook, pulled it on and tied the sash around her waist.

The upstairs was quiet and Andrea tiptoed along the corridor so as not to disturb Nancy and Rosemary Collins. She didn't want to run the risk of a late-night chitchat with Nancy. At the bottom of the stairs was the soft yellow glow from one of the suspended gold lamps always left on in the foyer. As her bare foot touched the rug covering the ground floor, the Irish setter came padding out of the living room, his feathery, red gold tail wagging slightly in greeting.

Andrea had been positive that John had gone to his room, but the presence of Shawn indicated otherwise. As she peered into the darkened room, there was no discernible shape that she could identify as John. Then the dog ambled down the hallway leading to the master suite. Andrea decided that he must have been wandering through the house and that she had been right in believing John was in bed.

Hurrying slightly, Andrea moved toward the foyer table and the small package from the pharmacy still sitting on its top. As her hand reached to pick up the packet containing the bottle of sleeping pills, she caught a glimpse of an unfamiliar object out of the corner of her eye. A sideways glance of investigation focused on a raincoat hanging on the coat tree, droplets of water still clinging to its waterproof exterior.

Pivoting sharply, she stared toward the living room and into Tell's impassive expression as he stood in the darkened doorway. Her heart stopped completely in an instant of disbelief.

"What are you doing here?" she breathed.

"I came back," Tell answered simply as if he had intended to all along.

As he stepped farther into the light of the foyer, the yellow glow marked the contrast of the white of his shirt and the teak brown of his tanned skin. A striped tie of gold and brown was draped around his neck, the top buttons of his shirt were undone. His black hair gleamed with dampness, accenting the raven sheen and shading his face.

"Why?" Andrea whispered, wondering if he enjoyed tormenting her.

Her hazel eyes grew large with pain and confusion. At least she understood why the dog had been in the living room. He had obviously heard the late-night arrival of Tell and had wandered around the house to investigate.

Tell shrugged, his unrevealing eyes never leaving her stricken face. "What are you doing downstairs?" A hint of impatience at her appearance underlined his question.

Breaking free of his compelling gaze, Andrea picked up the packet with the tablets from the small table, clutching it in her hands in front of her as if it were a shield.

"I left this downstairs," she explained tautly.

"What is it?" Tell demanded.

"It's a prescription ... I filled." She stared down at the packet, breathing in deeply to steady her trembling voice.

"For what?"

Tucking a dark blond curl behind her ear, Andrea fored herself to meet his gaze, sensing by the hardness of his tone that he wouldn't allow her to evade his question a second time.

"It's sleeping pills," she answered stiffly.

Long strides eliminated the distance between them before she could take more than one step backward. The packet was wrenched from her grasp and held beyond the reach of her hands.

"Give that back to me!" The command was rasped

153

hoarsely from her throat. Andrea avoided any direct physical contact with Tell. To touch him would destroy her fragile defenses.

Long fingers closed around the packet containing the bottle of pills and thrust it in his pocket. "You don't need them," he said firmly.

"Why did you come back?" A desperate, surging anger made her lash out at him. "Was it just to torment me more? To make me more miserable than I already am? If that's your plan, you've succeeded."

"Do you think I wanted to come back?" His mouth thinned harshly as he spun away and stalked to the living room as if he could no longer bear the sight of her.

Helpless frustration and the irresistible need to be near him carried Andrea into the room after Tell. "Then why did you come?" she protested. "No one expected you!"

A light was switched on, illuminating his rigidly erect back and squared shoulders. Tell replied without turning to look at her, "I came back because I couldn't stay away and I should be damned for saying it aloud," he answered in a low, cutting voice, lowering his head and rubbing the back of his neck tiredly.

Andrea drew a quick, silent breath, her heart leaping at the admission that he was still attracted to her and dying a little at his hatred for the emotion he couldn't deny.

"When I didn't know where you were," Tell continued in a low, self-punishing tone, "I counted myself lucky because I wouldn't see you again. Now that I know

154

you're here, I can't seem to stay away from this place."

Slowly, he turned to face her, an angry hunger burning in his eyes at the sight of her, his expression etched by torment.

"So I guess the answer is 'yes,' I've come back to make you miserable." His voice rose as the intensity of his inner pain increased. "To make you as miserable as I am! To torment you with my nearness as you torment me! And yes, to hurt you, too!"

Andrea swayed toward him, wanting to rush into his arms. "It tears at me, too," she said. "I knew it was best that you leave, but I kept wishing you would come back if only for a moment."

"I've been here for hours," he said with a wry curl of his mouth that bordered on contempt for her statement.

"For hours?" That was impossible. He couldn't have been in the house without someone knowing he was there. "Where were you?"

"I was walking, trying to convince myself to leave. I saw Adam's truck in the driveway and I knew I was a fool to come back to be used by you."

"Oh, Tell," Andrea murmured in a choked voice. "You don't still believe there's something between Adam and me, do you? He's engaged to a girl that he loves very much. He's nothing more than a friend, more of John's than mine. Why can't you accept that it's the truth when I say that what you and I felt was something very special and rare? It's a feeling that I've never known before or since I met you. I haven't gone in search of anyone to replace it."

155

"Not even to your husband?" Tell retorted harshly. "Or wasn't I supposed to remember he exists?"

"He isn't really my husband." Frustration hunched her shoulders as she averted her gaze from his face, not certain she could endure the pain of another tearing argument with Tell.

"Don't mince words, Andrea," he frowned darkly. "You can't deny that you're married to him."

"But what you won't understand or let me explain is that it isn't really a marriage at all. It's a farce," she protested.

"That's the way *you* look at it," he interrupted.

"That isn't true." Andrea closed her eyes briefly. "I don't love John in a romantic way and he doesn't love me." Her voice was tired. The strain of the last months had taken away its force, but this time she was going to tell him the truth. She would not allow herself to be sidetracked by his questions. "It was never my intention to marry John, not for his money or any other selfish reason you want to think. It was his idea for us to get married."

"You can't have put up much of a fight or you wouldn't have married him," Tell observed dryly. "John is a big man. I'm sure you can shift all the blame on his shoulders. He's accustomed to carrying heavy burdens."

"Yes, John is a big man." As always when Tell included John in his attack against her, a proud defiance gave Andrea strength to protect the man who had given her so much for so little in return. "And I'm not trying

156

to blame anyone. I'm trying to do, Tell, is to explain what happened."

"By all means explain." His lip curled sarcastically. "That's all you've wanted to do, as if it will make any difference." The pain of longing and love flashed across his face. "As if anything will make any difference," he concluded. The torment of loving and hating that was love laced his voice.

"Shortly after I moved here when my parents died, some vicious gossip started about John and me. In an effort to stop those rumors, John suggested that we get married. Don't you see, Tell, it was to give me protection. Our marriage was a cloak of respectability for me." Andrea pleaded with him to understand.

"And the money?"

Andrea spun away from his taunting question. "I hate that word!"

"But not the things it can buy," he mocked.

"No, I don't hate the things it can buy." She laughed shortly and bitterly. "Because it can buy me sleeping pills to drug me into unconsciousness and keep me from dreaming of you."

"Damn you!" The hoarse imprecation whipped around her head. In the next instant, her wrist was seized and she was pulled around to face the glare of his angry gaze. "How can you expect me to forget this—that you're wearing another man's ring?"

A frozen stillness held him motionless as Tell twisted her wrist to bring her left hand into view and found himself staring at the engagement ring he had given her. The

157

lamplight played over the diamond facets, the shaft of the rainbow hues pinning his gaze.

An unnatural calm spread over Andrea. "I often wear it at night in the privacy of my room," she told him, "and stare at the empty pillow next to my own." Sighing, she glanced from his handsomely chiseled features to the ring that claimed his attention. "And I don't expect you to forget that John's ring belongs on my finger, but I expect you to understand how it got there."

Slowly, he let her hand return to her side, releasing his hold on her wrist as he took a step to the side. A frowning, confused look moved wearily over his face.

"I'm trying to understand, Andrea," Tell murmured, but the expressive shrug of his wide shoulders indicated his lack of complete success in the attempt.

With fingers that had grown cold with the hopelessness of her love, Andrea removed the ring and held it out to him.

"Here, it's time I gave it back to you," she said tightly. "I should have left it at the lodge desk with the note that you tore up without reading. Instead, I waited in the hall outside the lobby, hoping that when you'd read what I'd written, you might ask me to wear it with the blessing of your love instead of a curse."

His acceptance of the ring had been automatic, the brilliant colors of the diamond dying in the shadows of his open palm. The killing blow from the invisible knife in her heart didn't permit Andrea to speak as silently she turned away to seek the dubious refuge of her lonely room.

"Wait." His pained voice stopped her. "Don't go. Not yet, Andrea."

She couldn't turn around. The tears that had been denied her since his sudden departure now filled her eyes. What little dignity and pride she had left begged her not to let him see her tears.

"There isn't any point in staying," she answered in a low, quivering voice. "It's truly over between us now."

"I can't believe that," Tell's husky voice intoned, "or I still wouldn't want to hold you in my arms."

He was directly behind her. His hands touched her, drawing her shoulders against the hard muscles of his chest. A shiver of excruciating ecstacy quivered through her, the shock waves of physical contact with him undermining her resolve to leave him quickly.

"Don't ...." Her voice broke for an instant. "Don't make it difficult."

"Difficult?" He exhaled a short breath of bitterly wry amusement. "It's always been difficult to keep my hands off you. Why should now be any different?"

When his hands molded her closer to his male outline and Andrea felt his warm breath against her hair, she knew that in another minute she would be lost completely to the magic of his embrace.

"No!" Stepping quickly forward, she pivoted toward him to elude the light grasp of his hands.

He tipped his dark head to the side. "You're crying." Regret flickered in his dark-lashed eyes. "It hurts to see your tears as much as it hurts to know that you're married to another man when you should belong to me."

Andrea intended to run from him, but Tell's finger touched her cheek and followed the trail of the solitary tear that had slipped from her eyes. His touch felt like the gentlest thing she had ever known.

"Don't be gentle with me," she begged. "Please, Tell, don't be gentle. I can endure your mockery and your sarcasm, but not this."

Tell simply shook his head. "I'm not big enough to understand, and I'm not strong enough to stop loving you."

Her head was swimming dizzily with his nearness. A betraying light of hungry love burned in her hazel eyes, letting him see how susceptible she was to his caress. His hand curled around the back of her neck, pulling her toward him. Weakly, she strained against his arms, struggling to deny the wild, breathtaking beat of her own heart.

But her resistance faded swiftly as Tell folded her against the vigorously masculine outline of his lean body. She felt the acceleration of his heart beneath her hand and felt him shudder when she pliantly yielded to his embracing arms. Muffled endearments were murmured against the thickness of her hair, making the world spin crazily until Andrea no longer knew what was right or wrong.

She didn't know how long Tell held her in his arms, crushing her against him as if there was satisfaction in just holding her. And after all the time they had been apart mentally and physically, it was almost enough for her, too.

Then, slowly, his mouth began moving along her hair to her face and she knew the moment had to climax with the searing fire of his kiss. She moaned softly in protest at his slowness. His possessive kiss, when it came, was as glorious as she had known it would be, sensually exploring and masterful and driven by a thirsty passion that Andrea wanted to quench.

Her own cup of love was overflowing. Tell drank his fill from the nectar of her kisses, yet his unquenchable thirst kept him coming back for more. Andrea's desire never was emptied. Her hands were locked around his neck to keep him drinking from her cup. His own hands were kindling erotic fires along her back, waist and hips.

At last he dragged his mouth from her lips, burying his head in her throat and igniting more sparks of passion that traveled down the sensitive cord in her neck. The collar of her robe got in the way and he pushed the offending material aisde, taking the opportunity to explore her white shoulders and sending more shivers of desire down her spine.

"I love you, Tell," she whispered with aching longing. "I love you."

Drawing his head back, he studied her face with lazy thoroughness, the ardent fire in his half-closed eyes touching each beloved feature. His arms held her on tiptoe, taking her weight as if it were no more than a feather.

"And I love you." His deep voice caressed her. "Whenever you're in the vicinity, my temperature rises, whether there's ten feet of snow outside or spring blossoms. It's a fever that won't go away or diminish no matter what I do."

A barely stifled gasp split the air, cleaving a space between Andrea and Tell as she pulled guiltily free of his resisting arms. Nancy stood in the living-room doorway, her hand clasped tightly over her mouth.

Her luminous blue eyes focused accusingly on Andrea. "You're the one!" she gasped, drawing her hand away from her mouth and taking a step forward. "You're the one Tell met at Squaw Valley!"

Tell's arm reached out to circle Andrea's shoulder protectively, but she moved away from it into the shadows where she could hide her humiliation in the darkness until she could regain her composure.

"Nancy, this is personal," Tell spoke quietly but firmly, "between Andrea and myself."

"How can you say that?" his half-sister demanded. "I suspected who she was this afternoon when we were playing backgammon, but she cleverly convinced me that she hadn't seen you before. I was even beginning to think she was my friend." She stared at Andrea with hurt scorn. "And all the while, she was using me to get to you!"

"That's not true," Andrea protested, checking the tiny sob that tried to slip through with the last word.

"I believed that story you told me about why you married John. It was all lies, wasn't it?" Nancy accused, running a hand through her silken brown hair as if unable to believe all of this was happening. With a wretched cry, she turned on Tell. "How could you have fallen in love

162

with her when she was already married to John? You must have been insane!"

"If it's any of your business, I didn't know!" Tell snapped. He lit a cigarette and handed it to Andrea and lit another for himself.

"You're my brother and it is my business!" Nancy retorted.

"You're only making matters worse. Why don't you leave us alone?" Tell sent an impatient cloud of smoke into the air.

"I just heard you say not two minutes ago that you loved her. You're in love with the wife of our mother's best friend. How could anything be worse?"

"Nancy, please." The ashes fell from the burning tip of her cigarette as Andrea extended her hand in a beseeching gesture. "He didn't know who I was or even that I was married."

"You let him fall in love with you and didn't bother to let him know that somebody had a prior claim?" An incredulous astonishment covered his half-sister's face.

"I know it sounds unforgivable..." Andrea began.

"That's an understatement," Nancy observed dryly.

Andrea spun away, shakily carrying the cigarette to her trembling lips. The inhaled smoke only made her cough. "I meant to explain to him," she continued, snubbing the cigarette out in an ashtray, "but he found out before I even had the chance to begin the story."

"I'm surprised he didn't wring your damned neck!" Plainly indicating that if Nancy had been Tell, she would have.

"That's enough!" Tell ordered, flashing his sister a silencing look.

This time Andrea wasn't able to elude the arms that firmly encircled her. She held herself stiffly, unable to accept his protection from Nancy's slinging arrows.

"Wait a minute," Nancy said suddenly as a thought occurred to her. "A second ago you said Tell didn't know who you were. Are you saying that he didn't know you were John's wife even when he came here?"

"No, I didn't know," Tell answered for Andrea, tenderly wiping a tear from her cheek and gazing anxiously into her face, "any more than she knew I was Rosemary Collins's son."

"At least now I understand why you were so savagely bitter and sarcastic toward her. And to think I felt sorry for her," Nancy sighed. "After the way she has hurt you, for heaven's sake, why are you protecting her now?"

"Because, in spite of everything, I still love her." His voice was grim, but filled with conviction.

"But Andrea is married," she protested.

"Yes, I am married," Andrea spoke softly, heartbreak throbbing in her voice. "Yet neither of you seem to understand that it's only an arrangement. You both seem to think it's wrong that I fell in love when I'm already married, but it's what John wanted ... for me to find someone to love. He wouldn't call it being unfaithful."

"Andrea—" Tell tried to interrupt, but she wouldn't let him. She was determined to finish her story.

"And you just said that you loved me in spite of

everything. That means you love me even though you think I'm a money-hungry little tramp." Her chin quivered as she searched his face for some sign that his desire to protest was more than a token denial of her words. "What kind of love is that, Tell? Where there's no trust or respect? I love you completely and totally. The only regret I feel is that we've been pretending in front of everyone else that we're strangers." She turned her tear-filled eyes to Nancy. "I apologize for deceiving you, but we'd both carried the lie so far that I had no choice."

Nancy was silent, a shadow of doubt flashing across her expressive eyes, revealing the thought that her vindictive tongue might have been too hasty in condemning Andrea for her brother's sake.

"Please, Tell, let me go," Andrea begged. "I'm very tired."

In truth, she felt torn into a thousand tiny pieces. She barely had the strength to make the protesting twist that freed herself from his reluctant arms. She wasn't certain that she could put all the pieces together again, nor that she even wanted to try. Keeping her gaze averted from both of them, she moved slowly and painfully toward the door.

"Andrea, please, we have to talk," said Tell. "We can't leave it like this."

She paused, her eyes downcast, her head slightly turned in the direction of his voice. "This time, I think it's really true. There isn't any more to say. If I can't know all the facets of your love—pride, respect and trust—then I'm better off with nothing, and so are you."

Tell followed her to the foot of the staircase, but he made no further attempt to stop her. Every step away from him was an effort. The joy of loving they had shared only a short time before was something she never wanted to let go.

The knowledge that his dark eyes were following her every step was torture. She could feel his silent demand for her to return to his arms where she belonged, yet didn't belong. But this was one time she was certain that she had made the only choice available. She had told him the truth, not as succinctly as she would have liked, but it had been the truth.

Without the inducement of the sleeping pills, now in Tell's possession, Andrea lay awake in her bed, staring blankly at the ceiling, feeling the dampness on her cheeks moistening the pillow under her head. Half an hour later, she heard light, feminine footsteps coming up the stairs. Whatever discussion Nancy and Tell had been having was obviously concluded.

It hurt to know that she had alienated Nancy's friendship. She had guessed all along that Nancy would feel badly toward her if she ever found out that Andrea had been the girl at Squaw Valley, it was perfectly natural. She could hardly blame Nancy for turning against her considering the anguish she had caused Tell, but it was painful just the same.

Much, much, later, Tell's even tread sounded on the stairs. Without even trying, she could picture the weariness and defeat—and maybe a faint tinge of bitterness—that had to be in his face. His footsteps halted at the top of the stairs. Andrea held her breath, waiting for them to continue to his room.

Her shaking sigh when they started again was caught sharply back the instant she realized they were coming toward her room. She couldn't bear another confrontation with Tell tonight. Her love for him was so great that she was terrified that she might convince herself that it was enough.

When Tell hesitated outside her door, her heart pounded so heavily she was positive Tell could hear it in the hall. Rigidly, she held herself motionless, fearful of making the slightest noise. If he believed she were sleeping, he might go away.

A bitter laugh tried to escape her mouth, born in the faint hysteria of the last thought. Sleep. How could Tell possibly believe she could sleep after denying the only man she had ever loved? Her teeth bit into her lip, drawing blood but succeeding in stifling the betraying sound.

When she felt she could endure the waiting no longer, his footsteps started again, this time away from her door. Seconds later she heard the quiet closing of the door to his own room. It wasn't a sigh of relief that she uttered but a choked sob of pain.

CHAPTER TEN

AT FIRST the knock on her door seemed to come from a great distance. The longer Andrea ignored it, the louder it became. Wearily, she opened her eyes, focusing them on the dim streamer of sunlight coming through her window. It couldn't possibly be morning already, she thought tiredly. She had only just fallen asleep. Her exhausted brain couldn't even remember what day of the week it was.

There was another persistent knock at her door. Andrea rolled on to her back, letting the heaviness of her lashes relax to cover tired eyes.

"Who is it?" she asked in irritation.

The only answer she received was the opening of the door. She frowned, opening her eyes listlessly to identify the culprit who had interrupted her sleep so early in the morning. All thought of sleep vanished completely. Was she dreaming, or was Tell standing beside her bed?

"Good morning." The vision spoke, proving he wasn't really a vision.

"What are you doing here?" she breathed her astonishment.

The expression carved on his leanly handsome features was resolute and hard but his dark eyes were gentle as they moved over her face. The memory of last night came flooding back and Andrea turned her head quickly aside, pulling the covers around her chest like a wounded animal wanting only to hide.

"Please leave, Tell," Andrea whispered achingly.

"No," was his firm and unequivocal reply. The edge of the bed took his weight and Andrea closed her eyes tightly against the intoxicating sight of him. "I love you, Andrea, and I can't accept your decision last night as being final."

"It has to be." All the hurt and torment returned anew.

"I don't see it that way, unless—" Tell paused "—unless you aren't in love with me and are seeking an excuse to end things."

"How can you say...." Andrea jerked her head around, her eyes, wide and tortured, denying immediately that there was any truth to his words.

Then she saw the complacent smile curving his masculine mouth and crinkling the corners of his eyes in the way she adored. Her heart somersaulted under his devastating smile. He had been teasing, not accusing or mocking.

"You see, Andrea my darling," the loving light remained in his gaze as he studied her face as if he would never grow tired of looking at it, "neither one of us can deny how much we love each other. That's quite a foundation to build on, isn't it?"

"No." Andrea wasn't sure what she was saying no to, but it was imperative that she utter some negative sound or she would yield to his persuasion.

His smile deepened at her puny attempt to argue. She

started to turn her head away, but he captured her chin in his fingers and refused to let her avoid him.

"I walked away from you twice," Tell said. "I won't do it again and I won't let you go away from me."

"No," Andrea protested automatically.

He tipped his head to one side, a hint of determination in his smile. "You're going to have to stop saying that word."

"No," she repeated weakly.

"Yes," he said firmly.

His mouth descended onto hers, taking her lips in a sweetly possessive kiss that was tender and firm. Andrea was unable to check her response, letting her lips move lovingly against his to deepen the kiss. She had neither the strength nor the will to deny the power of his touch.

"How can you possibly deny this, let alone forget it?" Tell asked as his mouth followed the curve of her cheek to her ear.

Tongues of hot lightening flashed through her veins, his sensuous caress making her skin tingle with longing. Her hands touched his chest, knowing they had been ordered to push him away and unable to obey.

"I can't," she moaned, "but—"

He kissed her hard and long, shutting off the protest she would have made against her own admission. Her breath came in shaking gasps when he finally lifted his head, to gaze into her love-soft eyes with satisfaction.

"Are you going to keep fighting with me?" he asked with gentle mockery. "Because if you are, I feel I should warn you that your defences are in pretty sad shape."

"You're not being logical," Andrea murmured quietly into the warm curve of his chest, as her heart finally stopped racing.

"Now it's logic you want." His mouth curved with amusement. "Last night you asked me to have faith. I have faith."

"Blind faith?" Pain and sadness etched her questioning voice.

"Is there any other kind?" he countered lightly.

"Yes," she nodded slowly. "There's the faith that comes from understanding."

The amusement faded from his eyes as he held her gaze, a grimness tightening the line of his jaw. For what seemed like a long time, the only sound she heard was that of her own heartbeat.

"Tell?" Rosemary Collins's voice called from the hallway.

"Mother, wait a minute!" Andrea recognized the anxious voice giving the command as Nancy's.

The door to her bedroom was open. Tell hadn't closed it when he came in. Her hands found the strength to try to push him away, but he simply clasped them in his own, holding them tightly so she couldn't pull free.

"I love you, Andrea," he said, "I'm not ashamed to be seen with you."

"But your mother . . . ."

The quick footsteps of his mother had nearly reached her door. An instant later she appeared, a smile of surprise and welcome spreading across her face at the sight of her son.

"Nancy told me you'd come back," she began, then suddenly she seemed to realize that Tell was in Andrea's bedroom. "Is something wrong? Is Andrea... is she ill? What's wrong?"

There was a long pause before the last word was weakly murmured to end the question because Tell had carried Andrea's hands to his lips, pressing an intimate kiss on the inner wrist of each in full view of his mother's gaze. The dazed look of shock that halted Rosemary's movement into the room brought a twisting lump of pain in Andrea's throat.

"Other than a case of supreme stubbornness, Andrea is very well," Tell answered.

"I'm sorry," Nancy entered the room behind her mother, apology clouding her sad eyes as she sought Andrea's forgiveness. "I wanted to explain to mother in advance so it wouldn't be such a shock to her, but she didn't give me a chance."

"It's all right, Nancy," Tell assured her instead, releasing one of Andrea's hands and turning slightly on the bed to be more in line with his mother. "Come here, mother. I want you to meet Andrea Grant, who just happens to be the woman I love," he said in a matter-of-fact voice.

"But she's John's wife," Rosemary protested as if for a moment she believed that Tell might have forgotten that fact.

"Mrs. Collins," Andrea's voice was as icy cold as her heart had become at Tell's attempt to use his mother to trap her, "would you please ask your son to leave my

172

bedroom? I've asked him to go, but he just ignores me.''

A frown of confusion drew Rosemary Collins's eyebrows together as she glanced bewilderedly at her son.

"Andrea, don't do this," Nancy pleaded. "The things I said last night were wrong—I didn't know it then but I realize that now.''

"It's all right, Nancy," said Tell, waylaying his sister's protest in his behalf. "It's all out in the open now. I'll leave the room if that's what you want, Andrea, but I have no intention of getting out of your life. I think you should understand that.''

"Come on, mother." Nancy quietly guided the still dazed Mrs. Collins from the room.

Tell released Andrea's hand and walked as far as the door before turning around, a hard glint of ruthlessness in his eyes. She knew by the look on his face that the battle of wills wasn't over.

"Are you coming down for breakfast, or should I explain to John why you're hiding in your room?" A dark brow was arched arrogantly in her direction.

"No," she answered swiftly. "I'll be down, Tell, in a little while.''

The grooves near his mouth deepened with complacency. He knew, as Andrea did, that she wanted to be the one to explain the situation to John, to try to make him see just what had happened.

There was a brief nod of his head. "I'll see you downstairs.''

Was it a warning or a threat? Andrea couldn't decide as Tell closed the door behind him and she heard his footsteps receding along the outer corridor. Perhaps it was both.

Andrea took her time dressing, not just to prolong the moment when she had to go down. She remembered the male vigor that had surrounded Tell, the vitally refreshed air. Only a feminine version of the same could hope to stand up under the incredible onslaught of his masculinity.

The mirror's reflection was satisfying when she was through. The simply styled linen shift with its scalloped neckline and its color like a milky sky pointed out the golden highlights in her dark blond hair and the jade green flecks in her hazel eyes. These same eyes also held a troubled glow. They, and her heart, were the weakness in her armor.

After slowly descending the stairs, she walked to the breakfast room, taking deep steadying breaths to control the nervous fluctuation of her stomach. All three—Tell, Nancy and their mother—were seated around the table. Tell was calmly sipping a cup of coffee, not even glancing up when Andrea appeared in the doorway. Nancy's troubled expression seemed to echo her own feelings. Mrs. Collins appeared composed until Andrea noticed the nervous way her hands were picking at her napkin.

"Hasn't John come in yet?" Andrea murmured.

"Not yet," Nancy answered, glancing anxiously at her half-brother, who had leveled his gaze at Andrea but hadn't bothered to respond to her question. "Mrs. Davison said he would be here in a few minutes."

Reluctantly, Andrea came the rest of the way into the room. There was a chair vacant next to Nancy on the opposite end of the table from Tell. Ignoring the warming dishes that contained eggs and meat, Andrea poured a glass of orange juice and selected a sweet roll. Her rolling stomach didn't really want anything to eat, but she felt that she had to make the pretense if only for pride's sake.

"I'm sorry about last night," Nancy offered hesitantly in a low voice.

"I understand," Andrea answered self-consciously. "I don't blame you for jumping to conclusions after the way I deceived all of you."

"If you feel that way," Nancy began earnestly, still keeping her voice lowered in an attempt at privacy, "then why can't you understand what Tell is going through? He really loves you, Andie."

"Nancy, let her be for now," Tell broke in.

Andrea stiffened, her gaze bouncing away from the directness of his. "Are you letting the condemned eat a hearty meal?" There was a strange and haunting bitterness in her question.

"Condemned?" he challenged. "Is that the word you would use to describe a life with me?"

"Of course not," she murmured with a despairing sigh. In her nervousness the butter knife clattered against the saucer.

"Thank you." There was a mocking inclination of his dark head. "May I pour you a cup of coffee?"

"Please."

175

The whirr of the wheelchair sounded in the hallway outside the breakfast room. Tell held Andrea's gaze for a long moment, letting her break free when the flame-colored dog appeared in the doorway. The setter made an inspecting glance of the room, wagging his tail briefly at Andrea before looking back at his master.

"Good morning, everyone." John's cheerful voice sounded out of place in the room that had become per-meated with tension.

There were stilted echoes of his greeting by all except Tell, who responded naturally. After a few inquiries about their night's rest, John positioned his chair at the head of the table. Andrea quickly offered to dish his breakfast.

"I must admit, Tell," John said after Andrea had set his plate in front of him, "I was a little surprised when Mrs. Davison told me you'd returned."

"I don't know why you should be," Tell responded easily. "I did say I would be back if I could straighten out the few difficulties that had arisen."

"You did say that," John agreed as he spooned honey on his biscuit, "but I had the impression that maybe you didn't want to come back, from the last of the talks that we had."

"Where would you get an idea like that?" Despite his relaxed pose, Andrea noticed the watchful sharpening of his dark eyes as he returned John's glance.

"As I said, it was just an impression," John said shrugging. "Impressions can be misleading, but perhaps you've discovered that." Andrea's gaze darted quickly to

John. Had there been a hidden meaning to his statement? "We're all certainly glad you were able to come back, Tell. Isn't that right, Andie?" His warm gray eyes, innocently clear and without any perceptive sharpness, met her troubled look.

The taut muscles around her mouth could only manage a fleeting and somewhat tense smile. "Of course," she agreed quickly.

An uneasy silence followed. While John ate, the others displayed an unnatural interest in their coffee, staring at the dark liquid as if it were a crystal ball that could predict the future. As the silence stretched out, Andrea felt her nerves being drawn out by the heavy stillness.

"It was certainly thoughtful of you, Tell, to bring some of that California sunshine back with you," John said, glancing out the window where the sun was trying to peek through the broken cloud cover. "It's been rainy and gloomy around here for the past few days—ever since you left."

"I don't think I can take the credit for the sunshine," Tell replied, draining his cup and placing it on the saucer. "There was only fog and gloom in San Francisco while I was there."

"Andrea," John sighed, pushing his partially clean plate away from him, "I think you were too generous with your portions." A strip of bacon remained on the plate. He took it and gave it to the dog lying beside his chair, unaware of any tension in the room.

"Mr. Grant," the housekeeper's disapproving voice

came from the doorway into the kitchen, "how many times have I told you that you shouldn't be feeding that dog at the table? He gets crumbs all over the floor and grease, too. Do you have any idea how hard that is to clean up?"

"I'm sorry, Mrs. Davison," John smiled broadly, a mischievous light sparkling in his eyes. "I'll remember the next time. I think we're all finished." He glanced around the table to see if there were any objections to his statement. There were none. "Why don't you bring us some coffee in the living room?" Wiping his hands on the napkin and setting it on the table, he turned the chair away from the table. The dog immediately rose to his feet. "Shall we?"

John looked back at the others around the table, plainly indicating that he expected them to follow.

Reluctantly, Andrea became a part of the general exodus from the room. She wanted to ask to see John alone, but she was too self-conscious about her reason to make the request in front of the others. Absently, she chose a chair in the living room that set her apart from the others, an unconscious wish to be left out of the conversation, so she could have time to straighten out her thoughts.

"I have a little story I'd like to tell you," John announced when everyone was settled—as comfortably as the hovering tension would permit—and the housekeeper had brought in the coffee tray. "Andrea knows it. Perhaps some of you know part of it, but I think that all of you will probably find the whole story interesting and enlightening."

Idly, Andrea wondered which of the stories John intended to relate of the bygone days he had compiled for his book. He and Rosemary had reminisced so often in the past few days that she thought nothing of his statement.

"It concerns a friend of mine," John began. "We went to school together, but as often happens, life led us down separate paths once we graduated. We did keep in touch, though, and I was best man at his wedding. After I became confined to this—" he patted the arm of his wheelchair "—we didn't see each other quite so often. He and his wife had a little girl, a charming, beautiful creature with her mother's looks and her father's remarkable gift of giving unselfishly."

Captured by a frozen disbelief, Andrea slowly raised her eyes to John's face, unable to accept that he was actually talking about her. His eyes were gentle as they met her wary look.

"Several years ago," John went on quietly, "my friend discovered that his wife had cancer. I saw him often during that time, but never once did he ask for pity or exhibit any. I won't bore you by relating the whole tragedy of that time. It'll suffice to say that even though my friend spent every cent he had, sold everything he owned, borrowed against his insurance, and took advantage of every bit of medical knowledge and personnel that was available, in the end, cancer won. When he lost his wife, my friend seemed to lose his own battle with life.

179

One morning he simply didn't wake up. You can imagine the grief his daughter must have felt at losing both her beloved parents within the span of a few short and disastrous months."

Andrea bowed her head, aware of Mrs. Collins's shifting uncomfortably on the sofa and Nancy's commiserating look directed toward her. Through the screen of her lashes, she saw Tell intently studying John through the drifting smoke of his cigarette.

"At the time of her father's death, the girl was engaged, to a rather feckless young man as it turned out. After the funeral, I invited her to spend a few weeks here. It wasn't too great a distance for her fiancé to drive and she had no place to live. I didn't think she'd recovered sufficiently to get on with the business of making a living. Unfortunately, the separation from her boyfriend was not a case of absence making the heart grow fonder. He found someone else more available and more eager to have a good time, so he broke off their engagement less than a month after the funeral." John paused, quietly inspecting his audience. "I don't imagine you can appreciate how traumatic such a series of experiences can be, followed one after the other, unless you'd lived through it yourself."

"Please, John," Andrea whispered, not wanting him to continue.

"This isn't necessary," Tell added curtly.

"Oh, I believe it's very necessary," John disagreed with a wry twist of his mouth, and continued. "After her boyfriend's desertion, I invited her to stay as long as she wanted. At that point, I don't think she cared very much where she was. Unfortunately, the fact began to circulate that there was a beautiful young woman staying in my house and a lot of tawdry rumors began to circulate about her presence. I never exactly understood what they thought I was doing, maybe chasing her around the couch in my wheelchair. I expected the gossip to die, but strangely, it flourished even though it had nothing to feed on. She never said one word about it to me, but I began to feel responsible for adding needlessly to her suffering."

"Is that why you married her, John?" Rosemary inquired with a proud and disapproving tilt of her aristocratic chin.

"Not responsibility alone, Rosemary," he corrected. "There was concern for the daughter of an old friend, a fatherly affection for the girl herself, an anxiety about her future, and the very selfish discovery that someone needed me. Plus—" he breathed in deeply and scowled "—I was swayed by her assertion that she would never love anyone again; that she had lost the only man she could ever love, the fiance who had left her for someone else.

"I, too, had known such a love and, even though she was very young, I felt I had to consider the possibility that what she said was true. Under the combination of circumstances, I suggested that we be married. She didn't accept immediately, but I managed to persuade her of the practicality of my offer."

Viciously snubbing his cigarette out in the ashtray,

181

Tell pushed himself to his feet, moving impatiently away from the center of the room.

"I don't know what the point of all this is, John," Tell said curtly, "but if it's a subtle attempt to let us know that you're aware I'm in love with your wife, then let me admit it freely so we can conclude this discussion. I have a ring in my pocket that I tried to give Andrea earlier, and will do so again, if it's my intentions that concern you."

"Be patient, Tell." John met his glaring look evenly and calmly. "Your anger and the fact that the ring is not on Andrea's finger leads me to conclude that there's still some point of misunderstanding. I think you share my beliefs regarding the sanctity of marriage, Tell. That you have evidently discarded them because of your love for Andrea pleases me. If you will let me continue, you may find the rest of my story very informative."

"Do I have a choice?" Tell sighed in disgust.

John merely smiled and glanced toward Andrea's wan face. "As I said, Andrea did consent to marry me, but she made one stipulation that I wholeheartedly endorsed without questioning her reason. She asked that our wedding be a civil ceremony. It's as legally binding as any conducted by a minister. Only someone who had a very deep feeling about the permanency of sacred vows exchanged in God's House would appreciate the fine distinction between the two ceremonies. There was also the understanding between us that if, by chance, she ever found someone else she loved, I would very readily grant her an annulment."

182

He reached into the inner pocket of his jacket and withdrew a folded legal size document.

"Last December, when Andrea was on holiday in Lake Tahoe, I telephoned her. Am I mistaken in believing that you were the one I talked to first, Tell?" John asked.

"No, you're not," was the clipped answer.

"I could tell by Andrea's voice when she subsequently came on the line that she had found that special someone. Foolishly, she had neglected to mention me to you, but I was certain that if you loved her enough you would listen to her explanation—a tardy explanation, I'll admit. At that time I took the liberty of having the annulment papers drawn up—prematurely, as it turned out, but here they are."

"Were you aware I was the man all along?" Tell asked tersely, a pinched look on his face and agony in his voice.

"No. That was fate, I guess," John said and shrugged. "But I think I began to suspect shortly after you arrived that you and Andrea had known each other before. Last night ... well, your voices carried fairly clearly down the hall to my room."

He wheeled his chair to Andrea, handing her the document with a tender smile. Her trembling hands accepted it, her chin quivering at his unbelievable understanding and unshakable affection.

"Now!" John wheeled his chair sharply around to face the others, a broad smile sweeping his strong features. "If I've staged this correctly, Rosemary, this is the moment when you and I and Nancy are supposed to leave the room and let these two people be alone to work the rest of it out for themselves."

Aware of the room emptying except for herself and Tell, Andrea stared at the document clasped in her hands. The silence continued for an eternity of minutes with neither she nor Tell moving or speaking. Then the brown shine of his neatly polished shoes was before her downcast gaze.

"Here," Tell said stiffly.

His right hand was extended toward her. The diamond engagement ring she had returned to him last night was held between his thumb and forefinger. She looked at it blankly, then at his tightly controlled features.

"I think you should have the chance to throw it in my face for being such a fool!" The anger that glittered in his dark eyes was directed inward, berating himself for ever having doubted her. "I said I would never leave you because, in my arrogance, I thought my love gave me the right to stay. I was wrong. And I was wrong when I accused you of not having any respect for the sacredness of your marriage vows. Your respect is much deeper than mine."

A hard lump filled Andrea's throat, choking her so completely that she couldn't say the words that filled her heart. With her eyes fixed on his proud, handsome face, she slowly rose to her feet, ignoring the ring still outstretched toward her. A tear slipped from her lashes, then another, sliding unchecked down her cheeks as Tell frowned in pain at the sight of them.

Two shaking steps and her hands were curved around

his waist as her head found its resting place against his chest. A convulsive shudder trembled through him before his arms folded around her and she was crushed against his muscular leanness.

"Forgive me, darling," Andrea whispered against his throat.

"What is there to forgive?" he murmured thickly. "I'm the one who was blind."

"So was I. Don't you see, Tell? I was so busy trying to make you understand me that I didn't try to understand you or the way you were ready to compromise your principles because you loved me." Removing the birthstone ring which had been used as a wedding band, she held out her trembling hand to him. "Would you put it on for me?"

Carefully, he slipped the diamond solitaire onto her third finger. His mouth was straightly drawn, but the fine lines around his eyes were smiling.

"I would certainly like to turn you into a bigamist, Mrs. Grant," he teased huskily, then sighed, "but our church wedding will wait until you're legally free, which won't be too long, thanks to John."

"Yes, thanks to John," Andrea agreed. The warmth of his ring on her finger carried the fire of his love, and there was an answering fire in her heart.

"We have a lot to thank John for, both of us," Tell said, gazing deeply into her eyes, "but not right now."

Andrea met his lips halfway, sealing their silent promise to trust, respect, and love each other for the rest of their lives on earth.

The sun burst from behind a cloud, shining through the lace curtains to bathe the embracing couple in a golden glow. The light flashed over the diamond on her finger, sending a rainbow arc of promise from the circling band of gold.